Moggies in Space

Edited by Rita Beeman and C.V. Walter

COPYRIGHT

Contents

Introduction

THE MATTER OF WHETHER a dog or a cat is the better pet has been hotly debated among pet fanciers since time immemorial, but people who argue on behalf of the feline have many valid points in their favor. For example, for sheer majesty, it is difficult to argue the superiority of a big goofy dog when compared with the regal bearing of nearly any cat in the world. I can respect that. Mark Twain ventured that a human/cat hybrid would "improve man, but it would deteriorate the cat." Clearly, Twain thought more of cats than he did of people. Hemingway would surely agree with Twain, as he said that cats have "absolute emotional honesty" whereas humans hide their feelings. There is something to be said for knowing where one stands with a wild (or tame) animal. Despite their emotional forthrightness, cats maintain an air of mystery that is endlessly enthralling. Through cunning, hauteur, and physical prowess, cats have a way of ruling the roost.

There's no doubt about it: cats are brilliant. Did humans invent tables so cats would have something off which to knock things, preferably breakable objects, containers of liquids, or breakable containers of liquids? I'd like to think that cats would be eager to take credit for this invention, as they enjoy them so greatly. Cats also seem to know what humans want of them, but they definitely will only do precisely as they intended.

I learned of the vindictive spite of a cat when we visited Mom's friend Mary, many years ago, who warned us about the sour-tempered beast who allowed Mary to live under her roof. "Don't pet Magic. She hates everyone." The warning was well-founded: Magic made a habit of choosing a visitor of which to make an example. Mere moments after we were seated, Magic sashayed into the room, all sweetness and light, and proceeded to wrap herself around Dad's leg. As would any person, he thought he was the exception to Mary's admonition: clearly, Magic adored Dad. No sooner had he reached down to pet her than Magic began hissing and spitting, doing her lethal worst from five of her six ends. Dad managed to peel her off his leg with the assistance of our host, Bobby, who was Magic's minion. Orphaned in her first week, Magic had been hand-reared by Bobby, whom she manipulated into doing her bidding. In his hands, she was putty, but for all others, she saved her worst, which was diabolical. She knew what she was doing.

For stalking, there's little on earth to rival a cat on the prowl. Sharks could learn some tricks from cats. Large wild cats have been known to haul carcasses high into the trees, carcasses that far outweigh them. The roar of a lion is both chilling and awe-inspiring. We manage to see these creatures safely in the confines of zoos and nature preserves, but one would be foolish to not recognize that these animals are barely contained, and that we only got the best of them on the food chain situation because there are so many more of us. The miniature, "domesticated" versions of feline retain the memory of the wild beasts they were. They seem to know instinctively that the ancients deemed them gods, and they expect that we should recognize this fact, as well.

This anthology is in many ways a flight of fancy that explores the mystery and wonder that is the feline, domestic, wild, or hybridized. This group of stories represents a broad population of felines who are varying degrees of mysterious to the human characters therein. All are warriors in their way. They have jobs to do, and they do them well. Some just want a proper nap, and maybe to kill something small and furry. One thing is certain, though:

if the dog is man's best friend, the cat is man's best fiend. Or we are the pets of the best fiends. Tomayto, tomahto.

Rita Beeman, Texas, 2023

The Cat Who Talked Through Walls

RODNEY L. SMITH

IT WAS BITTERLY COLD, dark, and wet outside, as what passed for winter on Goliath sent its first rain-and-cold front south. The small black and grey tabby's options grew fewer as his pursuers closed in. He was miserable and scared and not afraid to admit it. Dashing from shadow to shadow, he looked for defensible ground that did not have water dripping on it. Four pursuers gave chase, all bigger, older, and meaner, determined to drive him from their territory or kill him.

The senior pursuer prowled the facility where the ships that descended from the sky landed and parked. He sniffed for the scent of his prey, but the rain and wind dispersed it, making their stalk almost impossible. They pressed on, anyway.

The tabby saw his tormentors as they scurried across an open space, seeking to cut him off from any escape. He could see the fence ahead, which separated the machines that landed vertically from those that landed horizontally.

Me running out of strength, options, and running room. Me know to stay back from the fence. Me will be surrounded, cut off, and pummeled until Me dead or so badly injured that Me would live out last hours in agony until the cold saps the life from Me. Why did my mother abandon Me? Me guess she couldn't take care of my six brothers and sisters any longer. Me was first to be let go. She trained Me to hunt on my own, then just didn't meet back up with Me after she sent Me out.

He needed a position so strong the four could not follow. He shivered, waited, and hoped. Almost at the limit of his endurance, he saw a shaft of light behind his hidey hole from beyond the fence.

"All right, all right, I'm taking out the garbage. Quit your bitchin'! Sheesh!" The human left the hatch open as he walked the forty feet to the trash receptacle.

The small tabby saw his salvation at hand and took it. He saw a small hole in the fence and ran with all his remaining strength. Seeing him, his pursuers turned to block his path through the fence. One ran beyond the hole to block his escape. One stopped fifteen feet out from the fence and held position to block that escape route. The leader was in hot pursuit and gaining.

The tabby ran as fast as he could, but they were better fed, in better shape, and only feet behind him. He scraped his side as he ran through the fence, but he was committed to getting through that hatch and into the machine. The fence saved him. He was bleeding, but he had been small enough to wiggle through. His pursuers were not.

Me shot through the open hatch and looked for a place to hide, skidding into the massive cargo compartment. There, Me find a long space between cargo containers, running as far back as Me could go. The fear washed out of system, along with the cold, and Me crash.

Something watched from a short distance. Something unique to Goliath. Something not a cat. It watched and decided something needed to be done about these predators, but not today. She had other babies to train and release. After she took care of her babies, she would deal with them. Yes, she would deal with them.

The bridge was a model of efficiency and order. Although there were only two people on watch, they carried out their duties in a calm, practiced manner, with very few wasted motions. First Mate Mary Bond and Chief Engineer Dave Jones had stood many a watch together during their time on various fleet ships. They were comfortable together like an old married couple would be. They just weren't old or a married couple.

"Mary, have you noticed if anyone cut themselves?"

"No. Why do you ask?"

"I saw a trail of blood drops from the galley to the cargo bay. I wondered if someone cut themselves in the galley."

"Ask Doc when he wakes up."

The former *Restorer*-class replenishment ship, *GRS Provider*, was recently rechristened as the *SS Provider* and was on course to Tangelon with a cargo of machine parts. She had been decommissioned and auctioned off to retired Captain Mark Graham after she was determined obsolete and excess to Fleet needs. Mark, tired of working for people inferior to him, gathered several like-minded friends and became his own boss.

"You want some coffee?" asked Dave.

"Yeah, pour this out and get me some fresh."

"Coming right up."

"Has Mark ever told you how he came up with enough money for the *Provider*?"

"Not in so many words, but he did capture three Onkaray ships on the lead-up to the Battle of Thurmunga's Lens, including a cruiser, destroyer and a frigate. The prize money on the cruiser was almost enough to afford the *Provider* by itself."

"He was lucky. Didn't they stop that prize ship program just after the battle?"

"Yeah, change of government, change of whose palms got greased. Politicians couldn't figure out how to personally profit from it, so they closed the whole program."

❧ ❧

Me wake to footstep sounds. Me still damp and cold, but no longer bleeding. Me listen as footsteps move from right to left and stop opposite the gap in cargo pods that was my refuge. Not knowing what kind of greeting to expect, Me ducked around a corner as the human knelt outside my escape tunnel. He then stood, dusted his knees, and walked off to the left. Me heard a hatch open, close, and then there was just the hum of machinery.

Me awake now and free of my pursuers. It was time to see to my welfare as Me start licking my fur. The wound was not deep and was almost already closed off. Me gud. Me has shelter of a sort. It be dry and safe and do for the time being. Just not very soft. Me need to find better accommodations. Me continued to bathe, drying off and cleaning small wound.

Then Me hear it, a small squeak. It come from a creature the size of a mouse, but with antennae where its ears should be, scurrying between the cargo crates. Me unsure what it was, but it smell like food. Me squat down ready to pounce as it slowly, cautiously approached. Me waited hungrily until it was a long leg's reach away.

Me will it closer. Instinct and Mom's training take over and Me land on top of it, grab it with my claws and bite it on the neck. It let out a startled squeak and died. Me waste no time and practically inhale the creature, leaving only the tail and guts. Me feel better right away, full stomach give warmth throughout Me body. Me finish interrupted bath, purr, and sleep.

❧ ❧

"Hey, Doc, who bled on the deck?"

'What do you mean, Dave?"

"There's a blood trail from the galley to the cargo bay."

"Nobody said anything to me. Show me."

They found the drops and followed them from the galley hatch to the cargo bay, where they disappeared.

Doc shone his light into the space between the cargo pods. "I suspect we have a stowaway."

"We need to coax it out of there before we reach Tangelon and the cargo handling system kicks in. The cargo bots won't be gentle or even activate the safety protocols over something that can move in a space that small."

"Do we still have those sardines that Wiley got from that Earth export store?"

"Yeah, and they still stink as bad."

❧❦

The captain initiated an all-hands weeklong quest to identify the stowaway and coax it out of its hiding spot. The first task was to identify the creature. Not much time would be spent on it if it was a Fomalhautian slug runner or any other unappealing or dangerous critter.

Amy, second engineer, closed off the aft cargo door, deployed a video array in the cargo bay, and got the first clear images of a cat. Planning ensued.

Here Me am, catchted by humans. How hoomiliatin'. Me had eaten all the mouse-like critters within safe return distance to my refuge, but me was still cold and hungry. The smell of the stuff in the tin was so gud it made mouth water and near-empty stomach rumble. It been quiet for some time. The smell made Me ache all over with hunger. Me left refuge and approached the tin. I sniffed and it drew Me near. It smelled so gud. I skittered back to Me refuge a few times to ensure it wasn't a trap. Hunger overcame my caution and Me go for the tin.

Me barely got one fish out when the crate's door slid closed behind me. Me screamed in full kitty righteous indignation. Me hiss, Me yell, Me spit, Me growl, all to no result. Me trapped!

Doc coaxed the hungry cat out and into a crate with a tin of very expensive imported sardines from Earth. The cat never would forgive Doc for that. He was quarantined for two weeks while Doc ran every test he could think of, finally announcing the cat healthy and free of all parasites and transmittable diseases. He did find an anomaly in the cat's genome which made him different from an Earthborn cat. Doc saw no harm in it. Two weeks of quarantine calmed him down, along with regular meals. The crew held a brief ceremony to introduce Provider's newest crew member.

The cat was a natural suck-up and soon wound up sleeping in the captain's lap during long watches. The crew solved the problem of the feline toilet by shredding old engineering manuals. The other stowaways solved the problem of what to feed him. Mary won the "name the kitten" contest with Sir Nolan of Goliath, or just plain Nolan for less formal occasions. As T. S. Elliot said, no one knew the name he called himself.

❦❦❦❦❦ ❦❦❦❦❦

As the cruise continued, Nolan continued to imprint on the crew more than the crew imprinted on him. He got to know the watch schedule and wandered the crew quarters, making sure all oncoming watch standers were awake and ready to stand watch. Some appreciated this furry wake-up call, some did not. Nolan appeased those that did not by putting on a one-kitty show of pure kitten energy. One technique he used to wear down the grouchiest crewmember was to bat an old sock around as if it was the Provider Cup winning goal, until he was worn out and camped on the grouch's lap, purring and snuggling. Few could withstand a full-on assault of pure Nolan, lying on his back, belly-begging-to-be-rubbed cuteness.

That, and his single-minded approach to ridding the ship of a Goliath-acquired vermin infestation, made him a valued crew member.

~~~~~~ ~~~~~~

The *Provider* went into orbit over Tangelon right on schedule and Wiley loaded the heaviest cargo—mining equipment for the copper mines and stone quarries—onto Bennie's transporter, a medium-sized cargo carrier more suitable to land on the planet's surface than the *Provider*. Nacho's transporter was sent to the main spaceport with cargo pods full of foodstuffs and luxury goods. The transporters were also good for landing on more primitive worlds without the facilities to handle a ship the size of *Provider*, and they saved fuel costs in not having to burn thrust to get *Provider's* mass back into orbit.

Five transporter trips in three days delivered and picked up all the cargo for this system. Some minor violations of Tangelon customs regs and extra terminal fees, as usual, were covered by fines and payments to the right officials, and they were released to their next port of call: Serenity Station.

Nolan's success at hunting resulted in him acquiring a very round belly, but that went away as the vermin population declined. Doc had purchased some cat food on Tangelon for the day he ran out of prey. That day came when Wiley discovered a cargo pod with a partial load of seed grain gnawed into and full of the Tangelon sand hoppers. He spaced the entire pod, then sealed and fumigated the hold. Nolan, with no prey left, had to learn to eat dry food. He quickly adapted and his bowls of food and water acquired a prominent place in the galley. Any silver showing on the bottom of the feed bowl got a loud *mrow* for some human to fill it up again, before the poor kitty starved. The feline customs and rituals must be observed.

Mark and Mary were on midwatch, which would have been midnight to morning if they were on solar time. Now it was just an arbitrary four-hour block of time. Nolan laid upside down in Mark's lap purring, getting a belly rub. All was right with Nolan's world.

Mary adjusted a NAVCOMP setting, making a miniscule change in their direction.

"Is something wrong with the navigation computer?" asked Mark.

Mary made another slight adjustment. "It slips on the Y-axis sometimes. I don't think anyone but me would notice or even care. If we ever must make an emergency jump and emerge inside a gas giant instead of open space, they would."

Nolan awoke with a shock because Mark, somehow, sent an image of the *Provider* being crushed by the internal pressures of a Saturn-like gas giant into Nolan's mind. He jumped, yowled, and ran under the weapons' console. Mark set his coffee down, having miraculously not dumped it in his lap, and watched an embarrassed Nolan slink out from under the console. He walked halfway back to Mark. A thought formed in Mark's mind. *"You scared Me. Me sorry."*

"Did you hear that?" Mark said, almost spitting out his coffee.

"Did I hear what?" Mary continued checking the Nav console for faults.

"It sounded like Nolan apologized to me."

"Didn't hear a thing, Captain. You're not getting spacey on me?"

Initially, Mark was the only one Nolan could or would communicate with, but eventually Wiley could. The crew stopped thinking Mark was going space-happy. Doc experimented with Nolan and the crew. Eventually, all could communicate with Nolan telepathically. It was mostly symbolic, at first, but expanded with practice, as Nolan learned what things were called, especially sardines, his favorite snack.

It soon became no biggie that the *Provider* had a telepathic cat. The crew vowed not to let outsiders know. Nolan was instructed to respect crew privacy, and he agreed. Doc found a reference in an old biology site about a cat-like creature native to Goliath called a moggie, which was rumored to have telepathic abilities that helped in hunting and was able to breed with Earth-domestic housecats, but could find no further data.

❧❧❧❧ ❧❧❧❧

A week out from Serenity Station, Mark called a crew meeting. They all gathered around the galley table, except Nolan, who wandered about until Mary offered her lap.

"Crew, we are approaching Serenity; however, it's anything but serene now. Pirates have moved into the sector and are making the run to the station hazardous. They're going after unarmed freighters at this time, which we are not, due to the Fleet leaving the weapons installed when they sold the *Provider* to me. We can stand off a pirate fighter swarm with our rapid-fire pulsed laser turrets. Our armor and shields can absorb a lot of hits since I upgraded the heat sinks. Our transporters, with their upgraded plasma cannons and turreted medium rail guns, have the capability to destroy pirate boarding craft before we must repel boarders. Finally, we have the on-axis heavy rail gun to take on anything not bigger than us.

"*Provider* was designed to survive in a fleet-on-fleet battle, which is a lot more than the pirates can bring to the fight. I called you all together to give you a choice: do we go to Serenity and possibly run a pirate blockade, or see if we can find another customer someplace else for Serenity's cargo of three electrical substations, at a loss, or just jettison it to make room for some other cargo? If we deliver our cargo, Serenity is willing to triple our usual freight rates. In addition, warehouses at Serenity Station are full to bursting. The floor is open for discussion."

Mary spoke first. "I fought in the Battle of Firmant on a frigate less well-armed than the *Provider*. Pirates don't scare me."

Doc shrugged. "I go where you go."

"Skipper, you steer, I'll keep us going," Dave replied.

Wiley interjected, "I want to fire the main rail gun at something big."

Amy also shrugged. "I'm in. *Provider* is my home. Got no place else to go. If the pirates want to get in our way, their mistake."

Bennie said, "As long as we test the weapons first. Wouldn't trust some Fleet loggie type to have done some midnight requisition, looking for spare parts."

"What are we waiting for?" Nacho put his two cents in. "I didn't sign up for fighting pirates—just considered it as other duties as assigned."

Rob asked, "Joe, do you have anything else on your calendar?"

"Me? No. How about you?"

"I thought I might stick around and kick pirate butt."

"Great idea. Mind if I tag along with you?"

"Pick your spot."

"Well, we've heard from everyone but Nolan. What say you, Nolan?"

Nolan, roused from his nap, saw everyone looking at him, jumped down from Mary's lap, and proceeded to play a fierce game of kitty against pirate with a balled-up sock.

"*Take dat, an' dat, an' dat, you nassy pirates! Whasis a pirates? Gimme sardine.*"

The captain smiled and others laughed. "Seems it's unanimous. Prepare for combat."

⁂

Ammo stocks were checked and test-fired. Fleet loggie types hated having to deal with partial or broken lots of ammo, so they often left it onboard decommissioned ships. Damage control stocks were placed where likely pirate boarding teams might attempt a hull breach. Cargo was moved around to make fighting positions and barricades. Guns and ammo caches were positioned around the ship so Joe and Rob could fight breaching parties if they got inside the ship. Bennie and Nacho engaged in dogfights to test their transporters' combat limits.

In three ship-days, Mark was satisfied with their progress and issued all crewmembers sidearms and spacesuits with tethers. They were to wear their suits until they docked at Serenity Station. He had the deck tie-downs painted yellow so that if there was a hull breach and catastrophic loss of pressure, the crew would have an easily visible place to snap on their tethers and not get swept out into space.

The captain spent the next day with Doc, trying to find an accommodation for Nolan, while the crew secured any loose items and ensured that liquids would not be floating around should the artificial gravity fail. Scouring the storage compartments all over the ship, Doc found an empty, airtight, transparent instrument storage container and had the engineers fit it with double oxygen tanks and a regulator, pressure-tested it, and knew better than to introduce Nolan to it without sardines. It was secured on the bridge atop the NAVCOMP cabinet, ready for Nolan to survive a hull breach, at minimum.

Entering the Serenity System's outermost planetary orbital disc, they were alert to any pirate action, but they missed a scout ship hiding in the outer edge of a Neptune-sized gas planet. It reported the *Provider's* arrival in the system to the pirate attack force waiting two planets closer to the system's star.

⁂

Mark knew a scout was out there somewhere. Pirate leaders were not master tacticians, preferring to use brute force rather than finesse. Mark had one last thing to do to be truly ready for the attack.

He keyed the intercom. "This is the captain."

Numerous eyes rolled each time he said that. "We are about to take on a barbaric foe, one that has no concept of mercy or civilized behavior. Their scout is reporting our heading and speed now. They are waiting for us two planets ahead because that's a distance far enough from the station that they figure the station's defense cutters can't launch and get there before they'll have defeated us, looted our cargo, and leave, never to be caught.

"My intent is to surprise them. I will approach at current speed until just opposite where they are waiting for us, then go to flank speed. This will separate their faster accelerating fighters from their larger boats and ships. Once we reach flank speed, I will rotate the ship end over end, so our topside anti-fighter turreted lasers and rail gun are all clear to engage their fighter swarm head-on. Wiley, this will be your chance to fire the railgun at anything big or acting heroic. Try to hit some of their plunder ships. That would hurt them the most. Our goal is to break them up, scatter them some. Then I'll flip us back and resume flank speed and see how close the station's cutters are.

"The pirates will then send their breach boats at us. Bennie and Nacho, those are yours. Keep them off us, but try not to get yourselves killed. Use the end-over-end trick. Keep them guessing. Rob and Joe, you will fight the inside battle. Kill anyone you don't recognize. Good luck. Show no mercy. Everyone, close your spacesuits, check each other, and strap yourself into an acceleration chair. I'll sound collision before I go to flank. That is all."

Nolan observed this from inside his case, into which he had been lured with sardines, until he fell into a deep chemically-induced sleep (Doc had found a formula for feline tranquilizer mist), at which point Mark activated the air supply and latched it closed. With luck, Nolan would sleep through this battle. Nolan looked like a cat taking a nap in an old-style lunchbox. Mark laughed and wrote **Do Not Eat!** on the outside.

❧❧❧❧❧ ❧❧❧❧❧

Onboard the pirate flagship, their commodore watched as his plan was about to go into effect. He counted down the seconds before his fighters would swarm out and first, disable any armaments. Second, they would take out the engines. Finally, the assault teams in their breach boats would subdue the crew while the plunder ships emptied their cargo holds. This would happen within thirty minutes, if all his people followed their training. His prey was in the jaws of his trap. It just required his order.

The order froze in his throat as he watched the freighter's engines come alive and the big ship move off at beyond the top speed of his plunder ships and even some of his capital ships, and it was still accelerating. "What the hell is going on here? Fighters, execute! Stop that ship! Take out its engines."

The fighters had a physics problem to solve. How do you intercept a ship that has a headstart and is accelerating away from you? It was already beyond the planned intercept point. Acceleration in a system requires burning fuel, of which fighters carry only so much. Mass usually favors the fighters because lighter ships accelerate faster. The answer is to punch it to max speed and hope you catch them before you run out of fuel. The fighter commander ordered a max speed tail chase after the *Provider*.

⊱♦♦♦♦♦ ♦♦♦♦♦⊰

"Serenity Approach Control, this the *SS Provider*. We are under attack by close to fifty hostiles just passing your fifth planet. Coordinates to follow. Request immediate assistance."

"*Provider*, this is approach control: we have our five revenue cutters outbound. Expected time of arrival is sixty Serenity minutes. Hang in there."

Mark looked at his first mate. "That's going to be a long hour."

⊱♦♦♦♦♦ ♦♦♦♦♦⊰

The *Provider's* sensors showed thirty pirate fighters of various makes and models. Some were relatively new and top of the line; others were barely combat-capable. Mark waited to execute his surprise move until he calculated when he would catch the nicely bunched-up fighters in the cloud of laser pulses his turrets would produce. Then the fixed railgun would send twenty-kilo kinetic and shrapnel rounds at them. The shrapnel would explode amid the fighters, ripping them apart. The kinetic rounds could punch through to the trailing combat and plunder ships.

Going mostly on instinct, Mark sounded the collision alarm and flipped the *Provider*. The ship groaned. As all turrets gained a clear field of fire, the auto-fire engaged. A cloud of laser pulses tore a swath through the swarm of fighters for five seconds. As it tumbled and lined up with the pursuers, kinetic projectiles from the fixed railgun flew at hypersonic speed through the swarm, slamming into the pirate combat ships. Wiley got lucky and punched three kinetic projectiles into the destroyer's bridge, making it combat ineffective.

"*Weeeeeee! Gimme sardine!*" Apparently, the feline sedative was short-lived, but still had a calming effect.

Mark flipped the ship again to put her on a direct course to the station and put the pedal to the metal, as the lyrics to a song on the intergalactic classic music channel went. Mark didn't know what it really meant, other than to burn fuel.

Ten fighters were either destroyed or disabled. Half were the newer models that had been in the lead. The remaining five were a mix of older and less capable ships. Ten ships were ten fewer they had to deal with.

Those ten fighters cost a good part of their lead, but the turrets kept picking off the survivors as they swarmed around the *Provider*. It was a slow process, and *Provider* took damage, too. She lost two turrets to their relentless fire. Mark rolled the ship so they would have no gaps in defensive fire to exploit. Two older fighters got raked by two turrets as they made a run-in at an apparent weak spot. *Provider* lost another turret, but there were fewer than ten fighters to deal with now, and one exploded in a bright orange blossom of flame every few minutes or so until there were no more left.

⚜ ⚜

Fear descended on the pirate flagship. The commodore had summarily executed the fighter commander for his failure, and even though the compartment had been cleaned, it still smelled of fresh blood.

The commodore ordered the four breaching boats released with strict orders to overpower the *Provider* while he took the remaining combat ships to circle around and hold off the revenue cutters from Serenity. The plunder ships trailed behind the *Provider*, waiting their turn. The breaching parties would enter the newcomer ship, kill all on board, commandeer the *Provider* and retrograde out of the solar system with the ship. They had less than an hour, so they burned maximum thrust to close with their quarry.

The remaining combat ships, a cruiser and two frigates (all overworked and undermaintained), pulled to starboard, accelerated past the *Provider* and exchanged a few salvos. Mark called Wiley.

"Wiley, I'm going to spin the ship to give you some targets. Railgun the hell out of the big guy. Go for their bridge. See if you can use the medium guns to pick off some of their gun mounts, then go for the frigates.

"Bennie and Nacho, release and take on the pirate breach boats. You have them outgunned, but they are faster and more maneuverable. Be careful of their tail gunner. I'm going to accelerate in a few minutes to increase our separation and give the cutters a chance to get here before the pirates get lucky and overwhelm us."

⳾⳾⳾⳾⳾ ⳾⳾⳾⳾⳾

The pirate breach boats and *Provider's* transporters hit free space within seconds of each other. While Wiley worked over the cruiser, Bennie and Nacho threw caution to the wind and ran full speed at the four breach boats. They destroyed or incapacitated three of the four while the fourth dodged laser and plasma charges, ending up in the relative safety of *Provider's* gun shadow. Two destroyed turrets gave a semi-protected place for them to escape Nacho and Bennie, where they quickly attached their maglock collar, burned a hole in *Provider's* hull, and pushed two breach squads through before Nacho destroyed their engines and rear hatch, closing off any reinforcement or escape. Now Mark had twenty-two pirates to clear off his ship.

"Plan Green. All hands, Plan Green."

⳾⳾⳾⳾⳾ ⳾⳾⳾⳾⳾

With that announcement, Wiley joined Mark on the bridge and fired the defensive battery from there. Mark maneuvered the ship and placed on standby an especially developed program of evasive maneuvers to keep the ship out of pirate hands if the bridge crew was incapacitated. Mary, Rob, and Joe met up with Doc and fell in on the first defensive barricade. Amy crawled silently through the duct work to where the hull had been breached. She found a lone pirate guarding the breach point, even though Nacho had destroyed the breach boat's rear hatch and engines.

Amy hit the release and dropped the duct vent on the pirate followed by a tank of expanding foam sealant. It sealed the hull breach and entombed the pirate in three cubic meters of foam. Satisfied the hull was airtight again, she reactivated the atmospheric generators, dropped down to the deck, and went looking for pirates with her carbine and a satchel full of hull-safe space grenades.

The atmospheric generator worked quickly to restore air in the ship. Between the sealed hatches and rapid response capability, it was but ten minutes before atmosphere was restored. Now Mary could hear the pirates coming.

❧❧❧❧❧ ❦❦❦❦❦

The senior pirate onboard the *Provider* took charge and ran toward the bridge, hoping to find a disorganized defense and an easy capture. That was not to be the case. His point assault team rounded a corner and ran headlong into a barricaded passageway and veteran defenders. It cost him three men. He left three men to hold the crew in place and backed up, looking for a better path to the bridge. He ran into Amy and her grenades. She took out five.

Doc, Joe, and Rob went looking for the pirates and found three of them bunched up in a passageway trying to decide on a course of action. One of the first rules of combat is don't bunch up. Violating that rule cost them another pirate.

These pirates were a diversion meant to hold the crew's attention while the other pirate squad applied a breaching charge to the bridge's aft bulkhead. Mark saw them on the passageway cameras and called Mary's team into the bridge. As the pirates were ready to set off the charge, Mark had Dave route ship's power through the deck grating in the passageway. The squad leader and the man who had carried the demo charges lit up like they had been struck by lightning. The charges went off with a sun-blinding light, partially offset by the camera's auto-dimming function.

Neither side was prepared to exploit the momentary advantage. The surviving pirates withdrew to reorganize. The bridge crew took position behind consoles and waited. Amy slipped past the pirates to the bridge and recruited Rob and Joe to hold a plasteel plate where the breaching charge cut through to the bridge, while she tacked it in place and then welded it for a secure bulkhead. Mark released Nolan to scout out the pirates' hideout. Having a telepathic cat might come in handy.

Meanwhile, Wiley was having some success against the third-generation cruiser, but he was putting a strain on the *Provider's* stabilizers and the shields. His attack plan against the cruiser had the *Provider* jinking around, with the two big ships straining to dogfight, which they were never designed for. The old plasma guns on the pirate cruiser had little effect on the fifth-generation logistics ship's shields, the plasma charges dissipating harmlessly through the hull and heat sinks.

The railgun was capable of punching through the cruiser's hull, but aiming the fixed gun by turning the ship required skill Mark did not yet possess. His goal was not to dogfight the old cruiser, but to delay it long enough for the revenue cutters to arrive.

⤜⤜⤜⤜ ⤛⤛⤛⤛

Nolan scurried from shadow to shadow, seeking out the pirates. He found half of them in the cargo bay talking into a box and relayed that to Mark.

"Nolan, have they said what their plan is?"

"It is something to do with engines and cargo bay. Nassy pirate say he not leave boxes behind."

"Mark, if they knock out our engines and get the cargo bay hatch open, they can evac their squad using a transport," Dave said. "They'll probably leave us a present, too, for being so cooperative."

"Dave, reinforce the hull integrity force field to max. Nolan, get up here on the double before they punch a hole in the hull and space you. Back in your box."

"Gimme sardine."

"Mary, take Nolan's box and meet him halfway. I don't want to lose him."

Mary grabbed the case, Rob, and Amy and went in search of Nolan. Nolan and Mary communicated, arranging a rendezvous point just forward of crew quarters. They joined up and Nolan tucked into his lunch box. They retraced their steps and were about to enter the bridge when Nolan sent a warning from Mark. It was too late. As they turned to take cover, four pirates rose up behind a barricade.

Mark apologized as the pirates took them all prisoner. "We were expecting you back and let our guard down. They came in just ahead of you and rushed us."

"What's in the case?" said the head pirate.

"Just my cat in his pressure case."

"Let me see. My wife has always wanted to travel with our cat, but worried about explosive decompression. Give me the case just in case there's a weapon in there. Ha ha, made a joke."

Mark sent to Nolan, *"When he opens the case, run under the engineering console. Let things calm down, then come out and push the red-lit button and the green-lit button on the engineering console. That will turn off stabilization and execute my special evasive maneuvers program. Warn the others that they should find something sturdy to hold onto."*

Silent nods went around the bridge as the pirate fiddled with the latches. Nolan came out hissing with claws bared. He bounced off the pirate's chest and ducked under the tactical console.

"Not very friendly, is he?"

Mary volunteered, "He's just scared. I am. Why should he be any different?"

The pirate laughed. "Yeah, why should he be any different?"

Mary thought, *"Now, Nolan!"*

Nolan jumped out from under the tactical console onto the engineering console and had to walk over the two buttons twice before he achieved the desired result. Collision sounded, and all hell broke loose. Weapons slid across the deck, dropped by friend and foe alike. Wiley was first to arm himself, and a burst of expertly aimed plasma took out all the pirates on the bridge. Mark slammed the bridge hatch shut and started locking out the remaining pirate-held compartments and shutting off life support to them.

The ship pinwheeling through space was more than enough to cause the pirates to give up the attempt on the *Provider*. The approaching flotilla made the pirate withdrawal a requirement. There was too much uncertainty sticking around.

"Bye bye, nassy pirates! Gimme sardine!"

The radio crackled to life and Lieutenant Commander Carston's voice broadcast, "*SS Provider*, this is Serenity Flotilla 61. Shut down any defensive programs and prepare to be boarded."

Mark replied, "Negative, Flotilla 61. Our situation is under control. You may board us once we are safely moored at Serenity Station. You will forgive us for not being too trusting at the moment."

"Okay, *Provider*, have it your way. Just don't make any sudden deviations from standard approach or we'll have to kill you."

"We just need to retrieve our transporters and we'll follow you in or vice versa."

"Docking Bay Ten. It's the one lit up like a cabaret marquee. We'll follow you in. The public will all be misdirected to number fourteen for crowd control purposes. You're quite the celebrities. Your fight was on all the channels. You and your crew probably won't be allowed to pay for a single drink—if you have alcoholic beverages in your cargo bays for sale. We've been a bit dry since the pirates blockaded us. Of course, the government will give you a heavily discounted rate on any repairs."

Mark smiled. "I'm sure your ratings shot through the roof, but there were several times when we could have used some help."

"Looks like your transporters are docked with your ship. Just follow the bright lights. Your ship is a godsend. The pirates had us under their thumb. Repair parts are available, but at exorbitant prices. Normal foodstuffs are considered luxuries. Luxury goods just don't exist.

"The pirates would loot a ship and, less than a week later, the goods would appear on the black market. People got used to dealing on the black market and you may see some haggling as the monied crowd tries to outbid the middle class for your goods."

Mark watched the shimmering effect as the outer door of Bay Ten opened and the forcefield met the open vacuum of space. He looked at the public throng on the observation deck outside Bay Fourteen trying to get a look at him and his crew, then keyed the intercom. "Change into your fancy ship uniform. It's showtime."

It wasn't exactly showtime for two weeks, after Customs found Nolan on board and quarantined the ship, but eventually the crew were on the morning TriVid shows all over the planet. Mary and Nolan exchanged thought messages throughout their interview segment and Nolan acted like a typical kitten. He was a total ham. Nolan and the entire crew were made honorary citizens of Serenity, even though there wasn't an advanced degree on the entire ship, a citizenship requirement.

⁂

The Serenity wholesalers bought out the entire cargo, even the battle-damaged wares, which still brought in top dollar. One entrepreneur bought the contents of Nolan's litterbox and had it sealed in individual epoxy blocks as mementoes of breaking the blockade. Everybody made money. The *Provider* was invited back anytime with no docking fees, duties, or taxes.

Nolan got all his required vaccines and Serenity became a regular stop for luxury goods. Nolan's avatar even became a cartoon TriVid star. Royalties for use of his name and likeness paid for numerous expensive ship upgrades and a lifetime supply of sardines. He grew fat and happy and lived a very long life.

The End

Biting Off More Than You Can Chew

PETER DELCROFT

Xochi checked her suit for the tenth time, going through the motions for what was to come. Her laz rifle was held in two of her arms; the other two would be occupied opening doors and throwing grenades, if need be, of which three sat on her belt for easy access. She kept catching herself double-checking the ordnance, afraid they would disappear. She would need them if it all went bad, because she was about to do one of those stupid jobs that her career path had sent her on—the one she hated most in the whole of the galaxy: she was about to board a potentially hostile vessel.

They were hitting a partially functional derelict, with two intact sections still holding air and one section exposed to the cold of space. The ship had been nearly ripped in half when whoever had attacked them had used a freaking lance battery to engage. From the looks of the wreckage left floating in an unstable orbit around the nearest gas giant, the thing had evidently scored a direct hit. It was a miracle that two of the sections even had power, let alone pressure.

Boarding a ship in space was terrifying, in the best of circumstances. When you boarded a manned ship, at least you had some idea of what was to come. For the most part, it usually involved brutal close-quarters gun fights, where any side could come out ahead, luck or skill taking the lead seemingly at random. She had watched a clean boarding action go to hell when one flash grenade bounced wrong, or when one command was lost during the chaos of combat. What they faced today was notably less dangerous than hitting a manned ship, but these circumstances were unique, enough to put all the marines on edge.

Overall, though, the job was worth it. Dangerous, but worth it. The Spacer's Guild could process the find. Xochi knew a hulk this size could produce an enormous number of credits from the right buyer. It just needed to be cleaned out first to ensure they could send in the proper recovery crews.

Their boarding shuttle made connection with the space hulk's side, magnets latching it into place. A wave of laz rifles priming filled the shuttle air with high shrills. Their unit commander, Lieutenant Cos'Cash, was back on the ship and yelling into their comms, getting everyone in position for the mission. Xochi was in the third squad, breaching with her companions and immediately heading towards Engineering. While she wasn't a sapper, per se, her squad leader, Kil'kor, was. She and the rest of the marines with him were mostly there for fire support.

The other two squads were headed to the sections that still had their pressure intact.

The bay doors opened, revealing a small section of the metal hull of the ship. Xochi grabbed the acetylene torch and began cutting a hole into the vessel, working quickly to ensure they weren't behind the other boarding crews. Timing was essential in an action like this. The gas ran out a little early, but some percussive persuasion got the chunk she had been working on loose enough to give them access. With a sucking hiss, all the air in their ship shot through the opening, taking the cut panel with it.

Her magnetic boots kept her stuck to the floor of the shuttle till the rush of air faded. Her squad was in the hostile reality of the cold of space. The only sound she heard was her own breathing and that of her squad over comms. Each one of them was in full vacc suit, save for the Gongon, because of the area they were searching. Gongon had evolved on a low-atmosphere world, so they could maintain themselves in an area with little to no atmosphere without a suit for far longer than any other galactic species due to their adapted hides. Portoid like her were one of the worst when exposed, and no one could do it forever, as the black is hostile to most life. Gongon were the champions of getting sucked into the black and surviving. This made them invaluable on these breaching jobs.

Xochi listened while she hopped in zero gravity to the other squads as they lit up the comms with news of their breach into the two sections that still had air and heat.

"Breaching the side, entry imminent." The voice cut out as sounds came over the comms of their entry. When the voice came back in, it sounded horrified. "What in all things, what is thi—"

The distinct sound of retching came over the comms before the user cut themselves off. Xochi and her squad all sat looking at each other, gazing around their relatively stable section with concern.

"Squad One, do you read me?" Lieutenant Cos'Cash barked in his heavily accented galactic common. The call was coming in from the *Oxturch's Hope*, cutting out slightly from the sheer number of bulkheads between it and Xochi's squad. The *Hope* was their home base, pride of the local chapter of The Spacer's Guild, and the launch vessel for all their boarding shuttles.

No response came. Another query was put out, and this time it was answered.

"We got a problem here, *Hope*." The voice that came through was the squad leader of Squad One, Hisxos. It sounded like he was holding back a little. "This ship wasn't flying with a clean manifest."

Xochi thought back to the call they had gotten on the scrap network, about a huge vessel just waiting for vultures to strip it. The *Hope* had been the largest independent vessel in the area likely to reach it before the government arrived to claim the property. Reports stated some pirates had caught it in the black without an escort and disabled it enough that no aid could reach it before it had been left to die, after being stripped, of course.

"This must have been a research or prison ship. There are cells all throughout this section, emitters for hard light barriers, the works! The cells are filled with beasties, all dead. There are also beasties lying about *outside* the cells, also dead. When the ship got hit, it seems that not all of the cells had their hardlight barrier remain functional, so a whole bunch got out."

Xochi bounced over in her section to a nearby crate, all the while keeping her focus on the comms chatter. She broke it open and found piles of dry food stuffed inside. Hopping over to another, she discovered that it contained medical supplies. Looking around at the total number of crates, it was enough to keep the *Hope* running for months.

"My theory is that a whole bunch of cells sustained damage in the pirate attack. Whatever they were transporting got out, and it got into the other cells. Awful-looking fights between some of the creatures, real cage matches. Some have bite marks on them, like they got chewed on. We will keep sweeping cells till we reach the end of our section."

"Squad Two: report."

"I'm sorry, sir, but it's much the same. If you told me this ship was used as a slaughterhouse, I would believe you without a second word."

"Explain, squad leader."

"Something got out here, as well, but instead of a few things, it looks like, well, like everything escaped all at once. All the doors seem to be open, making me feel like there was major malfunction. The melee that ensued must have been some brawl; it's hard to step without sliding in the gore. I see Quandarks, a large Cormouth with its serrated rows of teeth, I even see a bunch of the crew that must have been caught in the bloodbath. No survivors yet, but we will report when we can."

These ships must have been transporting a huge number of specimens. Since they were flying in the dark, outside normal star routes and without an escort, this must have been some government ship not working out in the open. Xochi glanced at the other crates. Popping open another revealed odd-looking frozen dried meats, probably meant for one of the exotic specimens onboard. There could be anything on the ship.

"Squad Three: report."

Kil'kor jumped on the mics as he pulled his head out of another crate he had been investigating. "It's all clear on our end, *Hope*, nothing jumping out at us. Seems like the mess is confined to the vacuum."

"Understood. Squad Three, please continue your sweep."

Kil'kor used hand signals to send her and the Gongon ahead. The two of them worked to breach and clear the next part of the ship, until they had reached the bulkhead and needed to start heading back.

"Squad leader Kil'kor, we saw nothing. Returning to you."

"Roger that. We are heading towards the intact section to assist Squads One and Two. Sap charges have been planted in Engineering. At the very least, the ship will not go nova on us."

Xochi breathed a sigh of relief, happy that little worry was no longer on the table. The good mood was swiftly gutted as the comms lit up with the voice of the first squad leader.

"*Hope*, we found Folmorians. Even worse news, something from the cells managed to kill them. Then it *ate* them."

Xochi felt the air change as her Gongon squadmate's posture moved from relaxed to tense. He knew just as well as she did what that news meant. Folmorians were one of the most reviled sentients in the galaxy. Not only did their culture revolve around a diehard warrior class, making them volatile allies, Folmorians ate their enemy dead. It was said their physiology would then shift somewhat, adapting them to new challenges and letting them grow. It had led to them being culled to near extinction by local galactic polities because of the risk they posed to other sentients, let alone the galaxy at large. Other more peace-faring space polities had objected, but they hadn't stepped in the way of the slaughter. It's hard to defend sentients that eat other sentients, after all. The shape the other squads had found the bodies in was the key, though. What happens when you eat a creature like a Folmorian?

"Wait, what was that?" The voice of the first squad leader cut across the comms, stopping her in her tracks.

"It looked like fur, but I can't be sure. It was moving really fas—"

Screams took the place of words. It was loud enough that Xochi was forced to mute the other squads to avoid having her sensory organs damaged. The *Hope* was screaming back, Lieutenant Cos'cash howling as he tried to drown out the wails with volume from his end. "REPORT, SQUAD ONE, REPORT!"

The screams continued. The chatter was hard to decipher, interspersed with laz rifle fire and the sounds of the boarding party dying.

By this point, she and the Gongon had forgotten their sweep and were rushing in the direction their companions had gone, back to the other sections of the ship. The sounds of their booted feet were silent on the metal, the lack of air in this section of ship providing no medium for the sound waves to travel through. They only had their ragged breathing echoing in their helmets for comfort.

Another voice, this one belonging to Squad Two's leader, cut in. "We are responding to comms loss from Squad One, *Hope*; report will be imminent."

More comms chatter came through from Squad Two, mostly regarding the positioning for the breach into the section with Squad One.

Their breach was announced and thirty seconds later they were in. Yelled commands from Squad Two pushed her on, spurring her to quicker movement. It wasn't long before it all went to hell again.

"Oh, gods, it moves so quickly!"

"Has anyone got a visual on it? It just took down Poro-lin!" Laz rifle bursts cut into the voice, only for it to be cut off by the sound of another scream.

"Where the hell is it?"

"Quinda, on your six, damn thing is about to pou—" Another scream, this one ending in a gurgle.

"Watch out for those claws! What in the hell is this thing? Is that camofla—" Whatever else was intended was lost in the screech of the comm cutting out.

Xochi felt perspiration in her suit, the sounds of death and fighting echoing in her sensory glands. Neither her nor her squadmate looked at one another; they just kept bouncing and leaping in zero gravity while maintaining their corners and keeping each other covered.

"Squad One: report."

"Squad Two: report."

The only sounds that came through the comms were the gut-wrenching sounds of chewing and tearing, accompanied by a deep rumbling sound, like a vehicle engine idling. All of this was followed by the tell-tale screech of the comms unit in the marine's helmet being crushed.

"Squad Three: report!"

Kil'kor chimed in, breathing steady. "Squad Leader Three reporting. What are your orders?"

"Enter and identify the reason for comms loss from the other squads. Weapons are hot. Wait for your squadmates before you breach, only enter as a group. Do you copy?"

When the *Hope* got a confirmation of assent from Kil'kor, Xochi and her squadmate started hurtling off walls, ignoring their corners and not caring about damaging their suits. She bounced off a few bulkheads, ensuring she would have a few bruises by the end of this, but speed was essential; no telling what they were heading into. When they arrived, they found Kil'kor and their other squadmate hunched over a tablet. Kil'kor looked up, then handed her the device.

"Here, take a look at this. I hacked into a computer in Engineering and pulled some of the onboard files. Take a look at the Folmorian entry; it should help us understand what's to come."

In short order, both she and the Gongon were perusing the files on the tablet. The report listed how many Folmorian specimens the ship had captured, only two, in this case, as well as the approximate physiology of each. One of them was known to shrink and grow itself at will, growing twice its normal size, while gaining musculature to compensate. The other had some sort of cloaking or camouflage. Its hide seemed to blend into the background, allowing it to hug the sides of objects and almost become one with them.

Of all the other files logs for specimens present, there was only one type of creature that Xochi didn't recognize from her time in school. The beast shown was quite small and frankly adorable. Especially its young, those eyes could melt any heart. The file claimed it was called a "Felis Catus," found in Sector 274.B.X.65, on some backwater wet world that no one ever paid attention to.

There was a report, some sort of biological survey or textbook that must have been acquired by the team that got the specimen. It likely came from the planet the "Felis Catus" had been taken from, then translated into galactic common. The pictures that accompanied were even cuter than those on file. Huge eyes and beautiful variations in fur color and length. They were supposed to be quite plentiful on their home planet. Xochi was just getting to the creature's noted behavior patterns when her squad leader piped up.

"Whatever is in there must be quite the predator. We can't take it lightly, especially if it can waste two squads of marines that fast." He grabbed the tablet from her and stashed it. "Sorry, Xochi, no time to waste. The report we had listed all the fauna onboard and their physiology, so factor in those abilities for the ones you read. Assume danger is always close, shoot on sight, and kill orders are in effect."

Kil'kor signaled her to punch in the codes to close off their chamber and pressurize it before they transferred over to the intact section to hunt the hunter. When the door snapped open, it was all Xochi could do to keep herself from filling her helmet with sick.

Gore was everywhere. Pieces of whatever beasts had been in the cells were scattered all about. You could almost trace the battles that went on, like a horrible crime scene. This creature slashed this one and felled it, only to be brought down by that one. Then it was killed by taking out another one, who only got five feet before collapsing itself. Everywhere you looked, battles between combatants from the cells could be sewed into a grand tapestry of violence. Each glance gave more evidence of the war that took place inside the hulk after the pirates finished their attacks and fled.

Speaking of the pirates, Xochi passed what were unmistakably fresh corpses that did not match any of the military scientists or security forces for a black ship like this. A nearby cut in the hull confirmed who they were. They had taken losses in the raid, more than she guessed they had expected to. This hulk was listed as a simple freight hauler. What a surprise they must have gotten.

Xochi's squad fanned out, keeping in pairs and searching the area with their tactical shoulder lights. It didn't take long before her companions found the evidence of Squad One. Scattered around on one of the walkways in front of a broken open cell were their remains. The four of them convened on the spot to investigate. That turned out to be the wrong move.

Out of nowhere, Kil'kor screamed, laz rifle firing uselessly as he was yanked upwards into the air. In the space above him, the air churned, like smoke and heat mixing to distort the air above a flame, outlining the form of a quadrupedal long-clawed monster. It had its jaws locked around the back of Kil'kor's neck. With a sickening crunch, Kil'kor went limp, then fell to the floor. It opened its huge mouth, rows of sharp fangs gleaming purple with his blood. Hunt successful, the creature used its Folmorian camouflage to fade back into the bulkhead and disappeared.

While it was fading, it looked over and made eye contact with Xochi. Those huge predator eyes froze her in place. An image of that cute creature from the report flashed in her mind, only larger. She knew then what had happened. She even remembered reading in the report that they were carnivores, known to eat any flesh available if they were getting hungry. One week of no food and lots of bodies around would have been a smorgasbord.

The squad unloaded laz fire into the space it had just been. Not a single shot hit home, instead sailing through empty air to collide with the bulkhead beyond.

Kil'kor laid in a heap, twitching and kicking his legs in the last of his death throes. The rest of the squad stood dumbfounded for a moment until their training kicked in and they rushed together, forming a triangle and going back-to-back to avoid another ambush.

Xochi was stunned. What she had seen was no normal "Felis Catus." It was easily ten times the size that was listed in the report. Its fangs and claws were longer. And that camouflage—how do you fight that? Xochi had seen creatures like it in zoos, blending into their environments to survive the rigors of the ecosystems. Xochi had never heard of it being used by a predator to hunt. Until now.

Xochi had acting seniority with the death of Kil'kor. A mixture of hand signals got everyone in sync, with her companions taking up proper defensive positions as they moved away from the ambush site. All of them were careful to keep everything around in quick laz shot range. Xochi could feel the sweat running down her body inside the suit, her multiple hearts racing fast enough that she was having trouble hearing the comms over the constant thrumming.

Movement in the corner of her eye sent her already harried pulse overboard. Screaming the whole while, she fired another salvo but did little but burn some holes in the bulkhead and a few cargo crates. Her twitch fire was accompanied by the panicked firing of her squadmates. The Gongon at her side was swinging its head around, trying to pick a target. It was only because Xochi was watching it that she saw the jump.

The outline of the creature was plain, as it descended from an upper balcony in a leap to land on the Gongon. It soared through the air, clearing thirty feet before hitting her squadmate. It immediately latched onto the alien's back, back feet kicking at the Gongon's scales and shredding them. The beast took several moments to rip into her crewmate before kicking off. In midair, the camouflage activated, and it faded back into the metal of the bulkhead. She heard a yowl as, finally, the salvo she shot out in response hit home. Xochi rushed to the spot and saw a bit of blood splatter, but no sign of the deadly creature.

"Squad Three: report."

Xochi fumbled at her helmet button, connecting only after a few wobbly presses. "Kil'kor is dead, *Hope*, as is M'copr. It doesn't matter how many credits this scrap may be worth; the situation is F.U.B.A.R. here and we need to get out. We are heading back to our shuttle and evacuating on the double."

They moved slowly, forced to walk to keep their backs from being exposed. Xochi reloaded her laz rifle, tossing the spent power pack away to clatter amongst the nearby crates. By sheer dumb luck, it hit something in midair, revealing the beast stalking alongside them in a lazy lope. Xochi felt her eyes meet the creature's. This time she reacted fast enough. She dived downwards as it pounced. Missing her, it landed on her last squadmate.

Xochi lit it up as best as she could in mid-pounce with her laz rifle, but before she could do much, her squadmate was under the creature and being torn to pieces.

Xochi picked herself up and ran towards the way she had come in, leaping to take cover behind a stack of crates. As she landed, she threw one of her grenades back the way she had come, despite her teammate on the ground nearby. Desperation does awful things to people.

The boom rocked the area. She used the time to keep running, hoping the creature had been shredded by the blast. Even if it wasn't out for good, another injury would at least slow it down. She needed more information on these things, something to help her survive.

Her mad dash got her a decent distance away from the blast site, with nothing following, as far as she could tell. The camouflage of the beast didn't make that a comforting feeling, to say the least, but she would cling to anything at this point. If she gave up hope, she might as well let it kill her.

Her scramble covered enough of the ship that she felt it was all right to slow down and use some time for recon. She brought the report back up, the one on the "Felis Catus" the ship had recovered. She hastily skimmed the biological information. Yep, definitely an ambush predator; she had picked that up herself. No sounds to announce a pounce. Apparently, they also liked to play with their food before going for the kill. Just great.

A small video came up of the "Felis Catus" hunting another fauna on their world. The pounce she had seen before was prevalent, catching the poor feathered flier before it could find the air and safety. She kept scrolling until one thing jumped out to her that she had missed: the report listed the ship as taking two "Felis Catus" specimens onboard, not just one.

Claws suddenly raked down her back, pain flaring white-hot as she reflexively dove away from the attack. In a fluid motion built through years of practice, she sprang back to her feet and started running. It hadn't moved from where it stood, claws dripping in her blood and fluids. Her suit sealed up the holes, humming out warnings as it did. That wouldn't work again. Its eyes were fixed on her helmet. It almost looked like it was smiling at her. She saw it get low to the ground, wiggle its back legs and posterior. Then its camouflage re-engaged, and it was gone.

At the same time, she felt her feet go out from under her as something heavy slammed into them and she hit the ground. She pushed the button to engage the rockets on her boots, sending her careening along the floor, gouging a line into the metal and spraying sparks as she rocketed along, crashing into a stack of nearby crates.

The yowl of pain from behind her sounded angry and frustrated; the fire from her feet must have burnt the bastard a little. She redirected the boots to push her out of the pile of crates and angled them so she was blasted up onto her feet, fuel running out just as it pulled her out of her prone position.

Metal sole hit metal floor and she was off at a dead sprint. Another grenade went over her shoulder. When she turned to survey the blast, she saw two separate smoky outlines moving along the corridor behind her. One was racing along the ground, the other along the *ceiling*. They both deftly avoided the blast, barely seeming to slow. Whatever mutations they had gained from eating the Folmorians were in full force as they hunted her through the skeleton of the research vessel.

Xochi screamed into her comms, telling them to have the shuttle ready for take-off when she got there. She wouldn't have time to operate the controls, so she wanted the bridge on the *Hope* to remote into the pilot seat and get that thing purring before she got there. Any time she gained might be what saved her life.

She didn't need to see them anymore to know they were following her. The sounds of metal tearing and rending under their claws as they chased Xochi through the hallways felt like running down the hallway to the executioner's block. She blindly tossed her last grenade behind her and almost cheered when she heard one of the beasties wail in pain when it went boom. Finally, something worked!

Rounding another corner put her within visual distance of one of the cuts leading to a shuttle the other squads had used to breach this section. She dived through the opening, coming up in a roll. She immediately poured fire into the gap to explain to her pursuers how bad of an idea following her would be.

"GO, GO, GO!" Xochi howled, pleading with the *Hope* to get the breaching shuttle moving. A lurch underneath her almost sent her down, but she steadied herself as the ship shoved off and moved away from space hulk's side, venting air as it did. Debris and bodies were shot out into the black in a torrent of air as the section began to depressurize. She kept a close watch, trying to spot one of the beasts at the exit until her own shuttle door closed. She slumped into a nearby chair and laid her laz rifle between her knees.

Xochi was about to take off her helmet when she heard an impact on the side of the shuttle. The *Hope* lit up her comms unit almost immediately.

"You have a stowaway Xochi, that nightmare beast is hanging on the side of your shuttle."

Xochi felt her hearts skip a beat, wondering how a 'Felis Catus' could survive the freezing temperatures of the black. Then she remembered it had eaten the Gongon.

"Xochi, we can't risk you bringing that thing back here. We are recalling all remaining shuttles to salvage them. Yours is compromised in the extreme. Get to a hatch and get out into the black. We're putting a lance battery shot through that shuttle to kill the mutant fauna. We'll give you a countdown till we have to fire."

"Ten."

Xochi didn't waste time arguing, hauling as fast as she could towards an emergency escape hatch.

"Nine."

Just as she was about to pop it, she hesitated.

"Eight."

What if it was close to the opening? Screw it, better than getting lanced. She reached for the handle.

"Seven."

Out of nowhere, claws ripped through the hatch, creating a large gap. The eyes of the creature were visible, hunger evident in the light reflected in the creature's eyes.

"Six."

The section she was in still had air before the rending. The sudden depressurization sent her careening into the hatch door, blasting it open and sending her out in the dark, cartwheeling end over end.

"Five."

Xochi tried to use her suit air jets to steady her, but ended up burning up most of her tank to even right herself in place. All fuel was gone from her boots, so she couldn't use those.

"Four."

Looking back at the shuttle slowly moving away from her, she watched as the creature prowled along the side, staring out towards her, its tail swishing and flicking at the loss of its prey.

"Three."

The lance battery maneuvered into position, powering and lighting up as it did.

"Two."

The creature glanced over to the *Hope*, its form lit up on the side of the shuttle by the glow of the battery. The creature then crawled inside the open hatch, likely to hide from a bit of the vacuum. Gongon genetics didn't make you immune, after all.

"One."

Xochi smiled, using the last bit of her air jets to fire her towards the *Hope*. Her only hope.

The lance fired and disintegrated most of the shuttle. The shot took the vessel in the stern. Flux-drive cores were obviously hit, as the vehicle imploded, then exploded. Xochi hit the side of the *Hope* and engaged her magnetic boots, scrambling with the last of her energy to avoid the shrapnel from the explosion. One piece pierced her shoulder, sending shooting pains through her and causing alarms to finally blare inside the suit, warning her of a potential lethal loss of internal vacuum from a breach.

Half-crawling, half-walking the last few meters to a safety hatch, Xochi yanked it open and dropped into the pressurization chamber. When she hit the ground, she rolled into the wall and smacked the pressure seal button to close off the upper hatch, then collapsed from the effort of it all.

❦❦❦❦❦ ❦❦❦❦❦

Xochi woke up to hands on every side, carrying her through the hallways of the *Hope* towards what she hoped was the med-bay. Lights flashed as they hurried along, voices half-heard as she slipped in and out of consciousness.

Alarms blared to her left, bringing her party to a stop. Hushed voices surrounded her. She could see through bleary vision that some of the crew were in suits, others in just their coveralls.

They talked of continuing, something about her condition. Others argued they might be needed at the docks. Survivors might have made it onto one of the shuttles before the Lieutenant called them back to the ship.

She tried to say there were no survivors, but it came out in a mumble. They must have hit her with a strong painkiller. It didn't matter, though: no one was really listening. They were far too wrapped up in their conversation.

"We have to go. Six people to carry just one of her is too much, even if she is a marine."

"She's too damn heavy in the vacc suit and we got no time to strip her. She'll die if we leave her here."

"Damnit. Then we'll just have to bring her with us."

Argument seemingly settled, the party turned, and the hallways shifted. Signs that were once indicating the med-bay were now all directing them to the cargo area. Xochi began to recognize more areas of the ship. She could tell they were fast approaching the dock where she would have berthed if she hadn't picked up the stowaway, where she had left with a full squad no more than thirty minutes before.

As they turned the final corner, the large cargo bay opened before them. It had tall fifteen-foot ceilings to accommodate even the biggest shipments. This helped the *Hope* stay in business. It was large enough that they could have ripped off parts of the research ship and taken them whole. Now, of the numerous bay doors, number Five was flashing to indicate a shuttle had just finished its docking procedure.

Medics and medical bots were on standby, holo-gurneys and emergency fluids stashed away in a few drones that buzzed and hovered overhead, keeping out of the way of the movements in the hold. With a hiss, the doors to the shuttle opened. There was nothing to be seen. No person emerged and none of her companions stumbled out.

Instead, Xochi felt her blood run cold as a smoky camouflage outline of a large "Felis Catus" slunk out. She tried to scream.

Instead, the rest of the crew did it for her.

The Great Ginger vs. the Space Abductors

URI KURLIANCHIK

BEING GINGER IS MORE than a race. It's a lifestyle.

Now, I'm not just ginger. I'm also white. I'm complex. I like people, especially little girls who play with me and old ladies who feed me. There're a couple of humans who live in a house surrounded by trees at the end of the street. They're okay, I guess; always drop food when cooking, especially when I bite their ankles.

However, I also like to stalk the night and hunt birds and rodents and show other cats who's the boss—

Oh sneeze! I should have started with that. I'm a cat.

I have a ginger back and a white belly. I'm larger than most cats, but not because I'm fat. I have the sharpest claws in town. I can bite painfully, too. Once, I killed a pigeon with a single bite. He was teasing me, so I guess the lesson here is that unless you want me to do some cat stuff to your face, you'd better not mess with me. What does it mean to mess with me? I don't know...try it and find out.

Cats. I can't stand cats. I hate black cats who crawl on their bellies and try to snatch bits of food from distracted humans. I hate white cats who strut about like they're royalty. We cats bow to no one. I hate tabby cats who live in garbage and smell like garbage and are garbage. I hate ginger cats because they're fat and lazy and stupid and eat things that cats shouldn't eat. I hate fawn cats because— Hm. I'm not sure what fawns cats are, but they're some kind of cat, so I hate them.

There. You can't call me racist. I hate everyone equally. If you're some kind of cat I missed, I apologize. I hate you, too.

Dogs are all right. Some are mean, but they're always tied to something so you can walk around them. I don't like how they bark. It's loud and it hurts my ears, but if I walk quietly, they don't notice me. There's one dog I like. She lets me sleep with her on cold days. If only she didn't try to groom me all the time. I'm a big cat. I can groom myself.

What else? Horses. I don't have an opinion on horses. Owls? They're cool.

Insects are delicious. Fun and delicious.

Rats? Hate those bastards. They are the reason I practice my pounce every night. If I see a rat, that bastard is going down.

Jackals? Nasty creatures, but they can't get through the fence. It's fun to tease them. I like the angry sounds they make. Boars? I sometimes see them through the fence. I don't think they know I exist. Just smaller horses, as far as I'm concerned.

I see you're getting bored. You didn't come here to listen to a cat lecture you about race relations in small towns. You came here to hear about the alien abduction. Okay, this is how it went.

The sun was setting. I remember this, because the old woman was trying to get the three little girls to climb out of a big puddle and get back into the house so she could put them in a smaller puddle. I guess the point is to slowly prepare them for the trauma of not being in any puddle at all, but what do I know? I'm just a cat.

The old woman was bleating, the girls were whining, and their mother, who I guess is the old woman's daughter, was snarling from the window.

It was very loud and very splashy. A lot of cats hate splashing, but I don't. Can be kinda fun on a hot day.

I was lying on the grass in the shadow of the jumpy thing (humans need a big sheet of taut fabric to jump well), chewing on a chicken leg I expropriated from a smaller cat and wondering if I should step in and set things straight. I was just about to do nothing at all when I noticed strange lights in the sky and realized that the ambiance was gone. Birds, insects, other cats, other girls fighting with their mothers or grandmothers...all gone!

I instantly knew this was a case of abduction.

How did I know this? Cats know more than you think. We're not stupid, or at least I'm not. I don't sniff catnip because I'm dumb. I sniff catnip because I'm weak. Are you happy now?

Okay, okay. I'm sorry I hissed on you. This won't happen again.

You see, it's not something I like to talk about, but when I was a kitten, I was abducted. Yeah, go ahead, laugh all you want, but I have proof.

One moment, I was sitting in the shadow of a garbage bin, waiting for the big cats to finish tearing up a bag to see if there was anything I could eat inside. Next, I saw some lights shining from above and felt constricted, like the whole world was closing around me, suffocating me. I tried to struggle, but I passed out.

I woke after what felt like just a few heartbeats, except it was already dark. The cats were gone and so was the bag. Even the eggshells and fish bones were gone. I was missing the whole evening!

Even worse, the tip of my ear was sliced off, but not like someone tore it with his claws or fangs or beak or whatever. It was a perfectly straight incision. I also felt, I don't know, altered? I don't know. I was never the same after it happened. Just thinking about that night makes my fur stand up.

Anyway, I saw these lights in the sky and instantly my tail blew like it does when jackals or dogs are nearby. I felt like everything had suddenly gotten lighter, like that feeling you get when you jump from a tall tree or people toss you out of the window, you know?

So yeah, I panicked. Wouldn't you? I ran away as fast as I could and slammed headfirst into something I couldn't smell or see. I hissed at it, I tried to bite it, but I could as well be fighting the wind— Um, which is something I did once...and won! Yes, one time I hissed at annoying wind, and it went away. True story.

Dazed from the collision, I turned around and noticed the girls and the old woman staring into the sky. The girl's mom was gone. Even her scent was gone.

Stupid humans. They should have fled, but instead they just went on gawking. That's the problem with humans; they're so big and strong that when they can't solve a problem by their bigness and strongness, they get more confused than a chameleon in a flowerpot.

Meanwhile, the wind started blowing harder, but it was a weird kind of wind; it felt like it was blowing from the grass upward instead of across the land. I felt this tugging on the tip of my tail, my ears, my whiskers, as if someone was trying to pick me up in the least pleasant way possible. Now, if you know cats, you know that you do not, I repeat, you *do not* touch our whiskers!

So yeah, I went blood simple and did something stupid. I started hissing like I never hissed before and tried to bite the wind. Okay, so that story about fighting the wind earlier? I may have exaggerated a little...I didn't win. You can't bite bad weather into good weather. Even humans can't do that.

While I was trying to fight the wind like some stupid dog, the old woman picked up a broom and tried hitting me, the old crone, even though I was trying to protect her! What can I say? No good deed goes unpunished. That's why we cats have trust issues.

So she swung her huge broom at me, and she would have smacked me, too, except the wind snatched the broom from her hands and sucked it upward, into the light in the sky. The girls started shrieking. It felt like knives in my ears. Little girls are even worse than barking dogs.

One of them jumped out of the puddle, a little girl, not much bigger than me, and also covered in stripes, and was sucked into the air. It reminded me of those roaring devices the humans use to suck uneaten kibble from the floor. By my claws, I hate those things! The noise they make is even worse than little girls.

The other girls, one with large spots and one plain, tried to grab their sister and were sucked into the air right after her. Their shrieking left my ears ringing and my brain hurting. By this point, the grandmother was also gone. I didn't even notice her abduction. Usually, I can hear a mouse fart from twenty leaps, but now I missed a huge human being sucked into the clouds.

I tried to jump over the green fence into the yard of the couple with the tasty ankles...which was when they got me, too.

Damn abductors. I hate them even more than cats.

I landed inside a cave that looked like an oversized stomach, except it was made from shiny metal instead of meat. Just like a stomach, this cave had passages going into dark places. How do I know what a stomach looks like? Some rat thought he was tough enough to steal my kibble. He ended up teaching me anatomy. Later in life, I learned that rats, pigeons, even cats—we're all basically the same inside—but not the three bastards I saw in front of me. They were weird!

They stood upright, just like humans, and had the same number of heads and limbs, but there, the similarity ended. One was sickly green and glowed. The other two were gray, like bad tuna that even a jackal won't eat, though they didn't smell like spoiled fish. They smelled like balloons, which, by the way, you are also not supposed to eat. Don't ask why I know this. Painful memory.

These creatures were smaller than humans, only twice as tall as I am when I get on my haunches. They also had very slender limbs with three digits each, ending in little pads, kinda like geckos. Or, as I like to call them: wall snacks.

The heads of these creatures were enormous, almost as big as their bodies. Their faces were as smooth as watermelons, and had tiny mouths without any teeth and huge black eyes without irises. Now, you know how whenever three or more humans are together, they're always covered in fabric, and if you jump on a human without fabric, you need to be really careful or they'll slap you? These guys had no fabric, only small patches on the backs of their heads, like, like... I don't know like what. I'm a cat.

The human females stood in the center of the room, ordered by height. They looked like they were sleeping with their eyes open. Usually, humans get this look when they stare at the flickering surfaces inside their homes or when spoken to by older humans for a long time. However, these humans looked even more dazed than normal, especially the one who was both a mother and a daughter. She even drooled a little.

In addition to the humans and the creatures, the cave was littered with all sorts of devices made from stone and metal; some of it flickering, some of it beeping, and some of it just icky. I can't go into more detail, because, again, I'm a cat.

The grays were smearing some kind of goo on the scruffs of the women while the green was illuminating them with what looked like a metal banana. Whenever one began to stir, he aimed it at her and she got dreamy again.

This was serious. I needed to get out!

However, great Bastet had other plans.

No, I didn't hiss this time. I'm not a moron.

However, I did fart. You see, that bad tuna I mentioned earlier, the one that even jackals wouldn't touch, well...I ate it.

I ate it all.

At this point, three pairs of black-on-black eyes were turned on me. One of the creatures reached for me, and I hissed at him to indicate that I won't have his disgusting gelatinous pads soiling my perfect coat. He didn't heed the hiss, so he got the scratch. I don't care if you're human, dog or Bastet herself; if you touch me when I don't feel like it, you're gonna bleed.

The creature drew his hand back while I bounced away. I tried running down one of the passages, but I ran into that invisible, odorless wall again. My head was starting to really hurt. I was ready to scratch someone's eyes out.

The gray cradled his hand and glared at me, just like humans do when I rightfully scratch them. He reached for some kind of a device that looked like a metal claw, but his green buddy raised his hand, as if commanding the gray to stop, and aimed his own banana at me. A beam of light came out of it. It was bright, but not painfully bright. It made me feel warm inside my head, like my thoughts were racing and bumping into each other, but maybe it was just the bad tuna, or running headfirst into a wall. Twice.

Honestly, I don't know what he expected was going to happen. I'm not a kitten. I don't have to chase every beam of light I see. I know what a laser is. I'm not stupid.

I ran for the other passage, easily bypassing the clumsy grays, but of course, it was blocked by an invisible wall. And no, I didn't knock my head a third time. I'm not a bird. I gave it a lick first. It tasted stupid.

Meanwhile, the girls began to stir, so one of the grays picked up a banana and shone on them. They slackened and got back to dreaming and drooling.

Ugh. Humans are so sloppy. One time, one of these girls touched me after she'd had ice-cream. Sweet Bastet, that was awful!

With the light still shining on me, I tried running up the wall, but it was too smooth. Meanwhile, the gray I scratched opened one of the big rocks and pulled out something that looked like a broom with a clawing tip instead of a spanking tip. Good luck matching celerity with a cat, moron. I can catch lasers. I'm literally faster than light!

I used the stick as a springboard and gave him a good scratch across his balloon-like face. His head didn't explode, but he did let go of the claw-stick and grabbed his face, which started oozing something black and foul. At this point, both his companions aimed their bananas at me, and I felt really hot inside my head, like I was sprinkled with some kind of evil catnip or something.

This only made me madder.

I pounced at the other gray and tried to scratch his eyes out. He parried me with his arm, but I bit him. I bit him so hard I can tell you what he tasted like. (Bad, in case you were wondering.)

He started waving his hand around, dropping his banana, and started sprinkling the human females with his black goo...at which point, they came to, and this madness got upgraded into a proper frenzy. Not since a human child vomited inside the jumping thing have I seen so much crazy all around.

The girls started wailing and kicking at the grays' shins and pinching on their torsos, their mother employed some kind of a sonic attack (sure made my head rattle) and *her* mother picked up the broomstick (the actual broomstick, not the one with the claw) and started swatting at the green, who scampered up the wall like a spooked gecko.

He aimed his banana at the mother of mothers, and she instantly dropped her broom and became dazed again. Meanwhile, her daughter picked up the claw-stick and tried hitting the gray cradling his bleeding arm. However, he quickly aimed his banana at her, and her eyes became glazed again. However-however, this time she was running, so the momentum carried her across the cave and onto a big stone with all sorts of glowing crystal poking from it. Right away, the cave started spinning like the inside of a washing machine.

Yes, I know what a washing machine is. It's one of my favorite things in the world, and no, it's not a pervy thing. I just appreciate its meditative and aesthetic qualities. If no one hits me with a broom, I can spend countless heartbeats watching a washing machine running.

Anyway, the cave started spinning, tossing women, girls and creatures not from this world like they were dirty fabrics. They all just screamed and tried to grab onto surfaces that were too smooth even for me to hold. I, however, am a cat, and can pounce and bounce like a god.

I used the woman's ample behind as a jumping thing and went for the green, the only one I didn't have a chance to maul yet. By this point, he realized his stupid banana had no effect on me, so he pulled out a different device, the one that looked like a metal claw. This one shot a narrow beam of light, as thin as a whisker, and I instantly felt searing pain in the tip of my ear.

Sneeze and diarrhea! Now both of my ears were missing their tips! What can I say? I came at him with everything I had.

With my fangs, I tore at his wrist until he dropped his claw. With my front paws, I dug deep grooves in his gelatinous flesh. With my hind claws...I don't have eyes in my butt, but I felt them connect with something, so they must have done some damage. I'm a cat. My body is a weapon.

At this point, I wasn't hissing. I was snarling like a cat fighting for his life, which I guess I was. Meanwhile, one of the grays managed to reach the big stone with the claw stick. He twisted one of the crystals, and the spinning instantly stopped, throwing me and the green across the room. I landed with the elegance of a cat. He smashed against the wall with the lack of elegance of someone who was not a cat.

However, while the first gray was fiddling with the crystals, and the second one held the women trapped inside a beam of light, the smallest girl, the one with the stripes, picked up the banana that the first gray had dropped and shone it at him. He went numb right away.

The girl giggled and started shooting beams in all directions, alternately paralyzing and freeing random greens, grays, girls, and women.

This bedlam was amusing to watch, but the green still had two eyes, which meant I still had a job to do. I turned toward the green bastard with my most feral grin and snarled like one of the great cats of yore. The creature reached for his metal claw, the one that sliced the tip of my ear earlier, but in all the spinning and tossing and brain-freezing, it'd rolled away under one of the stones.

He was now defenseless against my claws and fangs. I was ready to exact terrible vengeance for what he did to my perfect ear...so of course the bastard decided to cheat. He reached a hand behind his back and pressed the patch I mentioned earlier, the same kind they were trying to fit the humans with before I put the fear of the claw into the bastards.

Everything disappeared in an instant. One heartbeat, I was inside a smooth cave full of panicking humans, world-controlling stones, and ear-mutilating abductors. The next, the humans and I were just hanging in midair, higher than any tree in town.

Then we started falling.

༄༅ ༄༅

Now, I'm a cat. We know how to stick the landing. We even know how to land on a stick, so I wasn't worried about myself. The humans, though, I was sure they'd break all their bones upon impact. They can barely survive tripping on me. Falling from many times their height? Eh! Forget about it!

This thought made me sad, because it meant they'd never feed me or play with me or splash me again...and it's not like the males of the house would let me eat the dead females. Um, not that I would. I'm a cat, not a jackal. I don't eat roadkill. It's undignified.

However, and this is the point where I realized the true value of the jumping thing, the humans landed on the taut fabric one by one, the women screaming, the girls laughing. After sinking several tails deep into the fabric, they somersaulted out with almost feline grace, and landed on the grass in a heap, perhaps slightly bruised, but definitely not smashed. Even the oldest one seemed unharmed, though you'd never tell it by the amount of noise she was generating.

The males of the house ran to hug the females, and there was a lot of crying and kissing and blubbering. However, none of this was my concern, so I got back to gnawing on my chicken thigh, which remained just where I left it, except there were a few ants trying to rob me of my meal.

All in all, this was a strange afternoon.

Grey, the Vanquisher of Vipers

JOHN D. MARTIN

VIRAT PATEL WAS AWAKENED one early summer morning, not by the rose-colored light of a summer dawn in New Hyderabad on Herschel III, but by the sound of hideous, feline shrieks coming from outside the house. As he gathered his still-somnambulant faculties, those sounds were joined by the shouts of his son, Milo, and the cries of his daughter, Prija. Milo was pounding on the door as hard as he could.

"*Pita,*" the boy yelled repeatedly, "it's the chickens! Something's into the chickens! Grey's out there, too." From the tone of his son's voice, Virat could tell that the boy was both frightened and angry. Prija was only cry-wailing and begging for mama.

"Preeti, wake up, we have to get up," Virat said, turning to shake his still-sleeping wife awake. "There's something outside."

"Go away. It's still dark," she muttered drowsily. Then, as she slowly realized what he had said and she heard her daughter's wailing, Preeti shouted, "Why didn't you tell me she was scared?"

She bolted out of her bedclothes, climbed over Virat roughly to get free of the bed, and lunged for the door.

The twinge of irritation lasted a moment, but did not slow him down as he, too, threw off the light bed cover and sprang to his feet. While Preeti spoke to the children, Virat grabbed his u-coil pistol from the shelf nearest the bed. The sound from outside the house was dying down, but the chickens—buff-breasted prairie fowl native to Herschel III, only marginally domesticated, to tell the truth, and only superficially similar to the legendary domestic fowl of Earth—were still in a state of alarm.

"Your *pita's* going to deal with whatever it is," Virat assured his son, speaking calmly and confidently while Preeti soothed their near-panicked daughter. She had bent down to the children's level and was stroking Prija's hair, while Milo kept one arm protectively wrapped around his little sister's shoulders.

"How long ago did this start?" Virat asked.

"Four minutes, maybe only three," his son answered. "It might be a snake, like the one that bit *mata*. A viper. *Pita*, I am so scared. Maybe a viper got Grey."

"No, it didn't. Grey's just fine," Preeti assured him, though she did cast her husband a look that said, "*And if he isn't, don't you dare tell him the cat is dead.*"

Grey was their steel-and-smoke-colored Maine Coon, born of genuine Earth pedigree stock and now two years old. He had been an anniversary gift from Preeti's parents.

"Milo, don't be scared," said Virat, putting his hand on Milo's face. Preeti picked up their daughter, while Virat looked their son in the eyes. He saw the fear die down. "Stay with *mata* and your sister. Stay in our room and wait for me." He patted them each on the head. Then Preeti and the children dashed for the interior of their single-story farmhouse, while Virat walked at a quick but cautious pace to the front door and the yard beyond.

Emerging outdoors, he saw a mass of feathered carnage at the near end of the chicken yard, with the apparently uninjured prairie fowl all gathered in one clucking, gabbling huddle at the farthest corner from the house. Two of the birds had, in their panic, gotten aloft enough to clear the fence and were headed for the wheat field as fast as they could waddle. But Grey? Where was that cat?

Virat heard a yowl and a rustling sound and a loud, assertive feline growl to his right, toward the border between the farmyard and the wheatfield. He looked to the long, rectangular field of still-green, growing wheat and saw stalks part as the family's huge Maine Coon, Grey, emerged from the field. In his mouth the cat held a twitching reptile, a Grant's hooded viper. Known locally as the green devil snake, Grey held it in his clenched fangs. When Grey saw Virat, he shook the viper violently, growling even more loudly, until it stopped twitching. The moderately domesticated mini-panther carried its limp prey toward the house, trotting right past Virat without so much as a head bump against his leg, to deposit the vanquished reptile's carcass on the front step. Then he looked up at Virat with his golden eyes, cleaned his whiskers and meowed a long, rich vocalization that almost sounded like "hallo."

Virat sighed, flipped his pistol's safety back to locked position, bent his knees to a squat next to Grey, and extended his hand. Grey came toward him and head-butted his hand. The massive cat's purr was louder than the clucks and squawks from all of the still-fearful fowl.

"Good work, boy," Virat said to the cat. "Let's go brag about how you fearlessly crushed that green devil."

Virat stood and walked into the house, and as he passed the front step, Grey enthusiastically whapped his head against his owner's calf, then raced him inside.

"You can all come out now," he shouted to his family. "And we might as well get ready for the day. It'll be dawn in a quarter-hour."

The viper, and it had been a moderately large one, nearly a meter in length, had killed three chickens. Virat was only able to salvage one of the dead birds for meat and had put the other two on the burning pile at the far side of the property away from the field. That would keep the remains from attracting more vipers or other creatures that might be interested in carrion. Milo had helped his mother with plucking and dividing the dead chicken. Grey had watched the process with such great interest that Preeti had resorted to exiling him to the nursery with Prija. From the bits of their daughter's narrative they could overhear through the door, Virat and Preeti gathered that Prija was making the cat participate in a re-enactment of the governor's high tea. While the noble, long-suffering beast tolerated whatever indignities the toddler girl was inflicting on him, the Patel parents and Milo froze most of the meat in the cooling unit. A little later, Preeti was supervising Milo as the boy boiled the bones with the bits of meat still clinging to them into stock, while Virat gathered the unusable remains for burning, when there came a jaunty knock at the door.

"Jasper?" Virat shouted. He recognized that knock, and looked up from tying the waste together for the burning pile. He had called his old friend on the handheld as soon as time allowed, which had been just before noon.

"Uncle Jasp?" asked Milo, who stood at the stove, stirring the boiling chicken stock in the making. He glanced toward the door for a moment.

"We're in here," Preeti shouted.

"I'll be right out," Virat said loudly. Preeti looked up from supervising their son and smiled at him.

Virat strode to the door, carrying the bag full of feathers and other inedible remains destined for the burn pile. When he got outside, he found Jasper Collins, all two-meters-ten of him, standing by the front step. "Uncle Jasp," as the children called him, was dressed in work clothes, which at this time of year meant a short-sleeved madras shirt with red as the primary color, coarse grey pants of Herschelian cotton, and heavy boots of red elk leather.

"Guess vipers got some birds, all right," Jasper observed in a sour tone, pointing at the chicken-yard, which was now quiet but still showed traces of the early morning attack.

"I thought the charged fence would keep them out," Virat muttered. "Our cat got the damn thing as it was making its escape."

"Good to have a cat, but the only thing that'll keep them green devils out is a good, solid henhouse. On stilts. Kohli's and Greene's haven't lost any since they built theirs," Jasper said as they walked across the yard, past the large vehicle shed and the massive orange brick grain silo behind it.

"Well, can they pay for the materials? I've got poultry to replace. And with Preeti's medical costs? You know how it's been. Organ transplant, lost time on the farm, hiring robo-planters and operators to finish with the wheat. Milo and Prija... I couldn't leave them alone, then. I appreciate Janie coming over to watch the children toward the end of it, all the help you two have given, but long-term, we will need a veritably miraculous harvest to make up the losses. And that assumes the summer will be kind."

He threw the bag onto the burning pile, pulled an ignition cube out of his pocket, squeezed it till it got hot, and tossed it on the rubbish. The bird carcasses, wood shavings, piled-up bags of cloth and paper, caught fire almost immediately.

"The long-term solution, and I know you don't want me to say it..." Jasper looked down sheepishly instead of directly at his friend and neighbor.

"Is for us to move into town? Sell the land?" Virat asked, craning his neck to make eye contact with the red-haired giant.

"Not sell, no," Jasper answered. "You could run the farm remotely. Like Greene's. It would be safer."

Virat shook his head. "And I'd have to send bots out here to tend the fields or hire it done by people. Either way, it's money I don't have. Or I'd have to sell some of the land we bought together. Preeti and me."

Jasper put a massive hand on the smaller man's shoulder and closed his eyes. After a moment, he said, "That's a no? No blame for trying. Would you at least let me help with a henhouse?"

"What with? Would you supply the lumber?"

Jasper looked toward the far eastern range of the Patel farm, squinting and shielding his eyes in the bright Herschel sun.

"No, you would. Those violet spruce over east, past the garden? They make great framing wood."

ѯѱѱѱ ѱѱѱѯ

Later that same day, long after Jasper had marked the trees he would take and then gone, while Preeti was putting the children to bed, Virat sat on the ground in front of the house, facing west. He pulled his knees up to his chest and watched as the sun set. He enjoyed the solitude for A few moments, hearing only muted bits of the bedtime routine, complete with story, of course, coming from the children's room.

Then the house was silent for a while, until he heard his wife approach and open the door. He turned his head to look up as she sat down beside him, spreading out her blue-green skirt so that she didn't rest on it.

"Your cat saved our chickens today," he said to Preeti as she took his hand.

"Most of them, anyway," she said, and leaned against him.

"After saving you? I thought Grey had exhausted his heroic potential, but he's proven me wrong." Virat put his arm around her waist. "If he hadn't stood by you yowling, I wouldn't have found you in time."

Preeti closed her eyes as a pained look crossed her face. "Grey the lifesaver. I doubt my *pita* and *mata* thought he would ever be more than a lap cat."

They grew silent and listened to the Herschelian songbirds, mostly blue-tipped pipers and greater gold warblers, and to the last humming of the blue bees that were the main pollinators in the county of New Hyderabad, as the last rays of the sun faded into the silver-blue glow of twilight.

"You know," he began, "as the children grow, it's going to be lonely out here, so far from Jalal."

"Oh, the Collinses and Greenes aren't that far away. Five kilometers. A little less for Jasper and Jane."

"If we lived closer in, I could have gotten you to hospital faster. The venom wouldn't have spread so quickly. You wouldn't have needed a new heart." With each word he spoke, Virat could feel his pulse accelerate as he remembered the panicked rush to the skimmer, carrying Preeti's limp form, the terror-stricken drive to the county hospital in Jalal, the awful wait in the lobby of the emergency medical station. Preeti noticed the change in his voice and drew closer to him on the ground.

"These thoughts. Did Jasper put them in your head, or have they been troubling you all on their own?" Preeti asked.

"He did suggest it. And the henhouse." He smiled a little and she began stroking the back of his neck with her hand.

"We could consider it, but, Vir, I think..."

Preeti's sentence was interrupted by a loud feline war-shriek. The sound, followed by growling nearly as loud, came from behind the house, from the proximity of the garden between the Patel home and the now-thinned stand of spruce.

"Grey. Again," Virat said anxiously.

He was on his feet first, Preeti quick after him. As they raced around the building to the garden, they seized tools they had left leaning against the wall nearest the garden, Preeti taking a one-handed scythe and Virat a shovel.

"No! Stay back," Virat yelled at Preeti, as they were close enough to see the cause of the commotion.

They slowed as they crossed the line of tilled, turned earth that marked the boundary between their yard of mottled blue-green native grasses and their garden. From there, peering past the leafed and flowering melons toward the bean vines climbing their meter-high wooden poles, Virat and Preeti saw Grey, his back arched, ears back, tail whipping in fury, as he growled and faced a dark green viper at least half as large as the one he had vanquished that morning. The cat was facing them, the viper was facing the cat, its back to the Patels.

"Stay here. If it gets past me or Grey, kill it if you can. Run if you must," Virat whispered to Preeti. She nodded. He moved forward slowly and cautiously, shovel at the ready. The reptile reared up toward Grey, preparing to strike. The huge cat growled, hissed, and backed up sideways.

"Hey, back here," Virat shouted and stomped his right foot on the earth hard to distract the viper. It worked. The snake whipped around to confront the new threat, and in that instant, Grey was upon it, leaping through the air with a violent grace. He seized the viper by the back of the head as he came down on it. Grey shook it hard, released it, jumped back, and batted the now-twitching snake with the claws of his right forepaw before backing away from it, spine still arched, and hissed at the writhing, mortally wounded reptile. Virat didn't wait any longer, but stepped forward and brought the edge of the shovel down right behind the viper's hood, decapitating it. The scaled body from the neck backward kept thrashing and sprayed both blood and intestinal contents in every direction. Grey leaped back out of the way, taking refuge behind a half-grown melon plant. Virat was not quite as agile in his attempt to escape the spray, and his charcoal-colored work pants caught a blast of the flying ichor.

Perhaps a minute passed before the snake's headless cadaver stopped thrashing. Grey stalked cautiously around the dead thing, its head still clenched in his jaws. The snake's own maw was still open, though Virat noticed that its eyes had already taken on the dull glaze of death.

"Grey, come here, boy. Good cat," Preeti cooed, and lowered her scythe.

For a moment, Grey looked back and forth from the site of his kill to his mistress, still growling in a low tone. Then, as she repeated her calls, he seemed to break out of the haze of predatory instinct and become aware that his people were nearby. He dropped the snake head, virtually spitting it out, cleaned his whiskers, then sauntered over toward Preeti.

"You're all right?" Preeti asked her husband.

"*Ja*, except for the pants. What detergent do you use for snake slime?" Virat lowered the shovel and pointed at the besmeared trousers.

"None. We burn those," she replied.

He nodded. "Right, I'll add them to the pile, with this." He pointed at the reptilian remains with the shovel.

"Don't come into the house with them," Preeti admonished him. Then she bent and picked up Grey, and began stroking him under the furry chin, evoking very loud purring in response. Then a troubled look came across her face, and she said to Virat, "Two nights in a row, vipers."

"That is odd, and I hope it isn't a pattern," Virat said, heaving the dead snake corpse off the ground, balancing it across the wide blade of his implement. "Take Grey and get inside. Keep the inner and screen door closed till I knock."

❧❧❧❧❧ ❧❧❧❧❧

The next day, Jasper called early in the morning, letting the Patels know that he was coming with his hired man, Frank Strasser, to help him take the trees he had marked. They arrived two hours later in the Collins heavy cargo skimmer, and before the day was over, the three men and one boy with two motorsaws between them had felled, sectioned, and loaded the four violet spruce from the east end of the Patel farm, all intended for use in building the Patels a stilted henhouse. As Jasper and Frank were preparing to get in the skimmer and drive off with their cargo, Virat stopped his old friend.

"Assembly is going to take a week?" he asked Jasper.

Collins stopped in midstep on the sideboard of the skimmer. "At least. Why?"

"I thought of something while we were cutting the timber," he said. "Does Dsouza's Farm Supply have anything like an ultrasonic emitter that would keep snakes out in the meantime?"

Collins shook his head. "Not in stock. You'd be waiting two weeks, at least. It would have to come from Kaur City."

"Damn. It was worth asking. Thanks." Virat patted Jasper on the shoulder. "They've been coming down at sunset. Guess I will watch the birds for a couple of hours till you deliver. And for that, we can't thank you enough. We'll pay you for everything as soon as we can."

Jasper shook his head and smiled. "Don't. You introduced me to Janie, remember?"

They parted company. Jasper drove west on the dusty farm-to-city road, and Patel walked back to his family's house, hoping Preeti was making chicken and potato curry.

❧❧❧❧❧ ❧❧❧❧❧

Keeping watch over their endangered prairie chickens was more challenging and nerve-wracking than Virat expected. The first night, he and Grey sat on the step outside, watching the edge of the wheat field for signs of viper intrusion, and only twice did Grey sit up from his place at Virat's side, trot to the edge of the yard, stand up and look around, only for an indigo-stained warbler to fly up from the ground a few meters from the field's edge. Around midnight, Virat decided to retire and took the cat in with him.

The second night, Virat decided to sit outside alone, leaving the cat inside behind a closed screen and solid door, while he stared at the field, gun in hand. It was barely twenty minutes before sweat began to soak through his blue-green madras shirt and the back of his khaki workpants.

In the children's room, Milo was reading *The Adventures of Jared Thorne in the World-Warp* from his light-reader to an attentively listening Grey, giving special attention to the sparkly action scenes.

In the bathroom, Preeti was bathing Prija in the full-sized tub, the toddler girl having graduated from the antique-style wooden tub in early spring. Intending to bathe herself afterward, and not wanting to get her day clothes soaked by her daughter's enthusiastic splashing, young mother Patel was wearing only her peach-colored bathrobe. As she tried to calm Prija down from an enthusiastic round of "splash Mummy," she heard a soft thudding sound from the far wall, near the vent. Preeti turned her head to look in the direction of sound and what she saw paralyzed her with fear.

Another green devil. Another Grant's hooded viper. This one was at least a meter and a half long. It had dropped out of the vent near the ceiling on the far wall onto the hardwood bathroom floor. It appeared dazed from the fall for only a moment. Then it hissed, a foul and threatening sound, and turned to face the mother crouched next to the bathtub. It raised itself up, and Preeti clutched her naked daughter to her chest.

"Prija, be very quiet. Don't move," she whispered. Then she muttered to herself, "What have I got in here to hurt it with?" She saw nothing suitable, not even a brush or a broom. All the cleaning implements, chemicals, and haircare gear had been tidily stored away.

She was at least six steps away from the closed door. Why had she closed the door? And the fractions of seconds it would take to stand, turn and move with Prija clinging to her? What difference would they make? Sound could attract the viper, but it had already seen them.

"Virat. Milo. Virat! Someone open this door. Snake!" She yelled the words as loudly as she could without letting the panic she felt seep into her voice. As she spoke, she secured her hold on her daughter and steeled herself to leap into motion the moment the door behind her opened.

No more than three seconds passed before she heard the pounding of her son's footsteps in the hall beyond the door. Two seconds later came the banging of the front doors, then Virat's hurried steps rushing down the hall from the other direction. Milo reached the door first, flung it open, and Preeti sprang to her feet. She dashed, with the quietly whimpering Prija clinging tightly to her, and was out of the bathroom in five, not six steps. She almost collided with her husband, who stretched past her to grab the doorknob and slam the door tightly shut.

Virat threw his arms around his wife and daughter. Prija began to scream. Preeti attempted to calm her, and Virat asked her in a voice on the verge of unchecked fear, "Did it get you? Did it get you?"

"*Pita*, Grey!" shouted Milo.

From inside the bathroom, there came a nerve-searing feline shriek.

"Get to our room," Virat shouted at his wife and children. Preeti ran towards their bedroom, Prija in her arms and Milo close behind. All the seconds they were running, Virat could hear the third cat-against-viper struggle behind the wooden barrier. Only when he heard their bedroom door slam did he ready his pistol and kick the bathroom door open.

The tub was still full of water, and Prija's Squiddy Sam bath toy floated aimlessly amid the rapidly dissolving foam. On the floor in the middle of the room laid the eviscerated carcass of a large viper, its color slightly darker than that of the one he and Grey had vanquished in the garden. Next to it laid Grey, a bloody bite wound obvious on his shoulder. When he saw Virat, the noble cat tried to stand, hobbled a few unsteady steps, yowled, and collapsed, panting.

Virat laid his pistol down on the side table next to the vanity across the room from the tub. He opened the dressing closet, took out a blue towel, then hurried over to his family's wounded cat. Gently, he picked up Grey, slid the towel under him, then wrapped him in it.

"Preeti, get dressed. Get the handheld. Call Dr. Straub, then Collins. Grey's hurt, and we aren't staying here tonight. Tell Janie and Jasper we're coming over."

Minutes later, the Patel family hastily rushed out of their house, Preeti carrying Prija and Milo carrying the wounded Grey. They hopped in the family's passenger skimmer, took to the hard road, and Virat threw the throttle as far forward as it would go. Once on the road, Preeti called first the local veterinary, then their friends, telling the Collinses that they would be arriving in minutes, explaining as rapidly as she could their state and that of their animal. Behind her on the bench seat, Milo stroked their cat's head and sobbed.

❧❧❧❧❧❧ ❧❧❧❧❧

When they arrived at the Collinses, Jasper directed the Patels into the washroom and told Milo to put Grey on top of their laundry unit, while Janie, Jasper's younger, shorter and much darker-hued wife, took the now-sleeping Prija from Preeti's arms. Dr. Straub arrived less than a minute later, but to the Patels, even that interval seemed too long. Straub, a thin, dusty-haired man only a handspan shorter than Jasper, chased all but Preeti out of the claustrophobically small space, asking her to help him manage his feline patient. Jasper and Janie's son, Willie, soon found Milo and drew him off to talk about the latest exploits of their light-text hero, Jared Thorne, leaving Virat standing alone in the hall, hearing only snatches of the conversation between his wife and the veterinarian. Minutes passed before the door opened and Preeti beckoned him to come in.

The vet had come well-prepared and done what he could in the space available. Grey was lying flat on his side on top of the laundry unit, but lifted his head to look up as Virat entered the room. The wound on his shoulder had been shaved and bandaged. There was orange staining around the edge of the gauze.

"Iodine?" Virat asked.

"*Ja,*" Straub replied. "I would like to take him to the clinic to put him on IV hydration with antibiotics. I injected him with AVA..."

"What's AVA?" Virat asked.

"Adaptive Veterinary Antibiotic," Preeti explained. "Dr. Straub carries it everywhere."

"In small animal dosages, too," Straub added. "And I drugged him for the pain. I'm surprised he's this alert. You've got one tough cat there."

"Is he going to live? The children will lose their hearts if..." Virat began.

"Though I can't make any promises," Straub said, and turned to look at Grey, "I think he will. The viper that bit him? It's not the same sub-species as the one that bit your wife. Yes, I heard about it. Nearly everyone in town did."

Virat drew closer to Preeti and put his arm around her shoulder. They looked down at their cat, who looked up at them and closed his eyes, purring.

"Not the same sub-species? There are different ones, then?" Preeti asked.

"Correct," Straub responded as he removed his hygienic gloves. "There are at least three. The one that bit you, Ma'am Patel, had cardiotoxic venom. The most common kind has neurotoxic venom. But the third kind, that seems to be the one that bit Grey—" He patted the cat, who responded by raising his head enough to lick the veterinarian's hand weakly. "—It's the kind with the infectious bacterial bite. There were venomous animals on Earth that had this kind of bite, too. It's nasty, but it is less likely to be fatal if treated quickly. The neuro- and cardiotoxins...eh. You two know that story."

Preeti shuddered and Virat gripped her more tightly. After a moment, he spoke.

"Doctor, we've now had three of these devil snakes attack our property in five days. Why? Is it just the chickens being out in the open?"

"*Ja,* your birds will attract them, being easily accessible prey. They're probably after eggs and chicks," Straub answered, and as he did, he began putting his medical instruments back in their case. "But my thought is that you recently had a nest settle in near you."

"A nest," Virat muttered. "What we need to do is find the bloody nest and destroy it. As soon as possible. Tonight yet, if Jasp can help me."

"Oh, no, no." The veterinarian held up his hands. "When have they been attacking?"

"Early evening," Preeti answered. Then, as she looked from Virat to Dr. Straub, understanding dawned in her mind and spread to her face. "The hottest part of the day, this time of year."

"Right." Straub stabbed his right index finger at her. Looking at Virat, he said, "Wait until morning to go looking for that nest. When the night air cools, they'll retreat to it. And they'll be lethargic. Now, Ma'am Patel, can you help me get your cat into a carrier? I do think it best to take him to the clinic."

❧ ☙

The Collinses' house was larger than the Patels', and had a guest room with a couple's bed, where Virat and Preeti slept with Prija in a disused baby bed, which Janie brought in and placed next to the window. Virat rose before dawn, left the bed quietly so that he would not disturb his wife, and after a quick shower, he met Jasper in the kitchen. They ate a quick breakfast of smoked sausages and bread, along with cups of chava, the locally favored hot breakfast beverage. Their hunger abated and caffeine levels stabilized, the two men then went to the Collinses' media and data center access unit, which Jasper used to call up the topographical map for the Patels' farm.

"Now, if I were a green devil, where would I put my nest?" Jasper mused aloud as they gazed at the aerial view of the land around the Patel farmyard.

"They've been coming from the north, from somewhere in the big wheatfield," Virat said as his friend increased the magnification and moved the crosshairs of the digital image focus on the screen with his finger. He moved the focus steadily north from the image of the house until Virat told him to stop.

"There, that spot," he said, pointing at an area at the farthest north end of the field, near a stand of massive Herschelian black oaks. "Last night before I fell asleep, I looked up 'green vipers' in *Vallaprasad's Wildlife*

Compendium. It says they like to nest in lightly wooded areas or naturally occurring depressions, rock piles, and dry areas that afford natural cover."

Jasper nodded, then spoke. "That area looks promising. Just go there and shoot 'em all? All that we can find, anyway?"

"Unless you can call in an airstrike from the capital," Virat said mirthfully.

Jasper arched an eyebrow. "You know, I just might be able to," he ruminated aloud. "I've got a couple of tanks of skimmer fuel in the shed. Drop one of those on the nest, shoot it, boom. Dead snakies. Any survive, we shoot them, too."

"Can we do that without getting hit by flying rocks and bits of the tank?" Virat asked.

"Probably," Jasper answered. "The max elevation for my cargo skimmer is ten meters."

"That ought to be safe if we shoot at a distance of, say, seventy. With any decent rifle, a non-moving target. Not a problem."

"This is about killing the snakes?" came Milo's voice. Both men startled slightly, and Virat turned to regard his son crossly.

"Why aren't you still sleeping?" Virat asked his son.

"I heard you two talking," he answered. "But if you're going to kill those snakes, I want to help. One of those scaly devils bit *mata* and now her cat. I hate them."

"He can shoot, can't he?" Jasper asked, with a touch of challenge in his voice.

"Bet the farm I can shoot," Milo answered with enthusiasm.

"Milo, this will be dangerous. We might have to get down on the ground with the snakes. If one bit you, I...no."

"Vir," Jasper said, "every hero needs a weapons bearer. With you driving, me looking and then dropping the gas bottle, it'd be good to have a third as the shooter. Milo, can you handle a .32?"

"I usually shoot those fan-eared rats with *pita's* .25, but I sure could," Milo responded.

"All right, Milo." Virat spoke to his son in a grave voice. "You come, but if we leave the skimmer, you don't. You shoot only from the skimmer. Only. We'll bring high-gauge scatter guns for any that we can't get with the fire."

⁕⁂⁕ ⁕⁂⁕

An hour later, the men and Milo had loaded two shotguns, one for each of the adults, a rifle for the boy, and a red and yellow eighty-liter bottle of compressed grade A90 skimmer fuel into the Collinses' faded blue, light cargo skimmer. When Willie woke up and saw what Milo and the "big men" were doing, Jasper had to spend a few moments telling him that, no, he could not come along, because he was three years younger than Milo and couldn't shoot. After the disappointed eight-year-old ran into the house, the three got into the vehicle. Virat took the driver's position. He fired up the engine, then retracted the canopy so that they would be able to shoot when the time came. Jasper sat in the passenger's seat with the fuel cylinder beside him, and Milo clambered onto the narrow bench seat behind his "uncle." Just as dawn crept over the horizon, they were off on their viper-slaying mission.

Virat flew Jasper's cargo skimmer, staying five meters off the ground, due north of the house and toward the untilled land around the long, irregular stand of oaks at the far end of his family's property. Jasper, sitting in the passenger's seat, scanned the area of rocky ground beneath the scattered trees with powered, magnifying binoculars. He had been scrutinizing an irregular pile of rocks when he shouted, "There, under that sickly-looking oak. The tallest one," and pointed to the stones.

Virat had to take the skimmer out in a wider arc away from the trees, slow down, and approach again from the south. He brought the vehicle in at a height of three meters. When they were only twenty meters to the west of the rock pile, he could clearly see that this was indeed the nest of Grant's vipers Dr. Straub had predicted they would find. Some were lying on the rocks, some peeking out from among the confusion of broken stone, roots and fallen limbs.

"There, to the right and forward," Jasper shouted, and gestured until Virat confirmed with a nod and a word that he understood where his friend was pointing. "Take us in till we're right above that spot with the big, flat rock. The copper-colored one."

Virat steered the skimmer as Jasper directed him, bringing it to hover between two and three meters in the air, just above the largest visible group of the green devils. Four of them noticed and reared up, unsteady and lethargic in the cool air of the morning. When he judged he had his best angle, Jasper picked up the bottle of compressed fuel and heaved it out of the vehicle onto the rockpile below.

"Now back us up. Fast!" Jasper shouted. Virat complied and turned the skimmer around in a tighter arc, putting them at a good seventy-two meters, give or take, from the viper nest.

"Get a good, solid bead on the bottle through your scope, Milo. Don't fire until you've got it perfectly lined up," Virat instructed his son.

"Right, *pita,*" Milo acknowledged. He took careful aim at the red and yellow cylinder and fired. Twice. Nothing happened except that a trickle of liquid skimmer fuel began to leak out from the bullet holes and spread on the ground.

"Ah, damn," Jasper muttered. "Must not have been enough of a spark to set it off."

Virat thought for a minute. "Or there's not enough oxygen in the tank. Fire needs oxygen, right?"

"Yeah, and now that the fuel's on the ground..." Jasper paused.

"Should I shoot it again, Uncle Jasp?" Milo asked.

"No, I got me an idea," Jasper said, and reached into the skimmer's small storage compartment between the two front seats. He fished around in the compartment until he pulled out an emergency flare.

"Get us closer to that cylinder, so I light this candle and drop it right on the A90," Jasper instructed Virat.

"Have you got any more of those, in case you miss?" Virat asked.

"Should be two more in there," Jasper answered, taking the safety cap off the flare as he did.

"Should be," Milo muttered.

Virat ignored his son's snideness and brought the skimmer in under the lowest hanging branches and boughs of the tall, unhealthy-looking oak. Jasper leaned over the side, sighted carefully, lit the flare, and dropped it, dead center on the expanding pool of liquid A90. As hoped, the fuel ignited in a fireball, catching several snakes at once. The flame raced up the flow of the fuel until it reached the source.

Then the cylinder exploded, sending fragments of metal and stone flying toward father and son Patel and Jasper Collins faster than Virat could switch the motivator control to reverse and slide the accelerator bar forward. Fragments of rock and the cylinder's steel casing flew at them, catching Jasper in the chest and Milo in the face. At precisely the moment Virat slid the accelerator forward, a viper they had not seen, one that had been sunning itself on a branch above them, dropped right into the rear seat, almost landing on Milo.

"*Pita!*" the boy shouted. Virat let go of the steering control, grabbed the shotgun beside him, and brought the butt of the gun down on the head of an angry, thrashing green viper repeatedly. Milo drew himself up into a protective ball in the farthest corner of the rear bench seat, and from the corner of his eye, Virat saw Jasper lunge across the front seat of the vehicle to pull the accelerator back to zero and shift the motivator to "coast." The sudden change in vector and speed threw Milo none too gently into the back of Jasper's seat and sent both adults slamming hard against the front console.

For a moment, all three of them were stunned, and the only sounds anyone made were coughs and groans. Then Milo sat up, his hand over his nose now, which was bleeding profusely, as was the cut on his right cheek.

"*Pita,*" the boy said, "I think my nose is broken."

Virat looked at his son and saw Milo's injuries for the first time clearly. One second later, he noticed that they were still moving backwards on momentum and turned around to set the motivator to "station," stopping the vehicle. His back hurt where it had slammed into the steering control.

"Jasper, does this thing have a radio?" Virat asked.

The big man shook his head. "My handheld's in the box there, with the first-aid kit. Better get that out, too." As he spoke, he pointed at the compartment between their seats.

Virat retrieved the kit and the handheld, gave the latter to Jasper and opened the small black box with the Red Cross symbol on it, getting out gauze and absorbent wadding to treat Milo's injuries. He instructed his son to pack his nose and sprayed the cut with wound disinfectant before giving Milo a bandage to hold over the cut. Milo straightened up and pressed the bandage hard against his face. The backseat was a mess of snake blood, and the carcass laid on the floorboard. Virat picked it up and cast it angrily out of the vehicle. Only afterward did he turn to face his old friend again.

There was a pained grimace on Jasper's face, and he was rubbing his neck.

"What's wrong?" Virat asked.

"When we shot forward, it jerked my neck around real hard. Hurts like nothing has in ten years, maybe. Next time I say, 'Got me an idea'? Hit me." He tried to smile, but his face instead twitched into a scowl. He hit the start button on his handheld. "I'll call the...oh, damn. Virat, get us out of here."

Virat turned away from Milo to look in the direction of the tree and rockpile and saw the ground around the oak and the tree itself were ablaze. The fire was spreading.

"Whomever you're calling, add the fire brigade to the top of the list," Virat said. He turned around to face forward in the driver's seat and set the motivator to "forward," taking them toward the Patel house.

❧❧❧❧❧ ❧❧❧❧❧

Jasper's handheld only picked up signal from a relay transmitter when they got within a hundred meters of the Patel farmyard. Calling the VFD of Jalal was initially fruitless. All of Jalal's volunteer firemen and first responders—the same people, all seven of them—were dealing with a vehicle collision on the far side of the county. The Jalal dispatcher routed them to the next available emergency responders, in Kaur City. It took their emergency vehicles, which were wheeled ICE trucks of an antique design, an hour to get to the farm. Virat winced as they tore through his wheatfield toward the qualm of smoke rising at the north end of the field.

Quick medical checks found that Milo's nose was broken and would need to be set. An application of wound seal and restorative cream dealt with the cut on his cheek in minutes. Virat's back was only bruised, nothing was broken, no ribs cracked. Jasper's case was the worst and took the longest. Virat watched nervously as the emergency medic looked at her own medical handheld and aimed the sensor wand at the back of his neck. Shaking her head, she yelled for her assistant to get a spinal collar out of their ambulance.

"What's the injury?" Jasper asked.

"Insult to your spinal column between the fifth and sixth cervical vertebrae," she said. "You're coming with us. For observation."

"Vir, can you tell Janie? And take the skimmer back?" the big man asked. Virat nodded.

Just then, the sound of the returning fire trucks drew Virat's attention. The plume of smoke in the distance was dissipating. That was a relief. The sour expression of the fire brigade's chief when he emerged from the lead vehicle, however, was a source of distress. The balding, heavyset man, face smeared with sweat and soot, walked directly toward Virat and Jasper.

"Mr. Patel?" the fire chief, whose name badge read "Kapoor," called.

"Yes?" said Virat.

The chief held out a handheld, bidding him to take it. Reading the text on the screen, Virat had to suppress a cry of outrage.

It was a bill for emergency services rendered.

"Read it through, and sign using the attached stylus," Chief Kapoor explained. "Note that we will be deducting the cost for damages our vehicles caused to your field. That will have to wait on an adjuster, but it's guaranteed. If the price of wheat is high enough in the fall, you might even get a refund."

"A refund," Virat said weakly. He was tempted to protest, but a furtive glance at the chief's face told him not to. He signed and handed the device back to the fire chief.

Another quarter-hour and the emergency vehicles left the Patel farm, headed up the farm-to-town road, the ambulance headed for the quickest route to Jalal. Virat and Milo stood next to the borrowed skimmer and watched them. Only then did Virat notice the wretched stench coming from the back of the Collinses' vehicle.

"Milo, let's clean this out," he said to his son. "And get that snake carcass out of the bathroom. It's quite ripe by now."

Cleaning out the skimmer took minutes, but removing the wretched stench of days-dead Grant's green viper from the bathroom required extracting and replacing a one-meter section of the pale blue tile with tiles of a much darker blue, the only suitable color available in the domestic goods store in Jalal. For the duration of that home restoration project, the Patels continued their sojourn at the Collins home. Janie welcomed their help during Jasper's extended convalescence, Jasper's spinal bruising having made him unable to turn or bend for most of two weeks.

In the meantime, Grey was returned from the veterinary clinic and, when the Patel children saw him emerge from the carrier into the Collinses' living room, Virat, who was repairing mesh screening on the henhouse project outdoors, could hear their cries of joy. With their mothers, they even held a "Welcome Home, Grey" party, serving the cat plain iced yoghurt with fish bits in it.

By the time Jasper was healed, the henhouse was finished and the Greenes, Collinses and Kholis worked together to bring the shelter for the Patels' chickens to its planned location. Not wanting to miss an opportunity for a community celebration, Virat and Preeti invited all of their benefactors to a garden party the week after midsummer.

Virat and Jasper stood at the edge of the wheat field. They looked out over the ruined swath left by the emergency vehicles toward the burned oak tree and the still-blackened ground around it.

"Wheat prices are rising, you know," Jasper commented. "You might get that miracle harvest in spite of this."

"*Ja*, I heard. Drought in New Mercia. Bad news for them, good news for us," Virat responded.

"You know what you need? I mean, for the northmost part of your property?" Jasper asked.

"Hours of work to clear it and make it suitable for planting?" Virat countered.

"No. Cattle. Or sheep," the taller man answered. "It could make great pasture. You wouldn't have to cut down the trees or clear the stones."

They walked idly down the path a few meters. "We did get rid of the snakes," Virat said. "None since we acted on your idea. Consequently, I'm not going to hit you."

There was a rustling sound to their left, and Grey emerged from the now-yellowing wheat. He had something small and furry in his mouth, and when he saw the men, he trotted over to them and deposited his prize before them. Virat and Jasper saw that it was a fan-eared deer rat.

"Oh, so the mighty vanquisher of vipers is a mouser now?" Virat asked the cat.

Grey replied by flopping down on his side and rolling.

Guardian Angel

B.A. IRONWOOD

I WASN'T SURE WHAT woke me up. One moment, I was asleep next to a warm wall, and the next, I was on all four paws, hissing at nothing. My dreams had been unsettled, full of teeth and claws, and the sense that something stalked me in the shadows. I still felt as though someone had rubbed the fur on my back the wrong way, and I spent a moment grooming myself to calm down. I decided to leave my hiding place, intending to seek the comfort of my humans.

The metal was cool to my paws as I patrolled my home. I could hear the quiet hum of the place, feeling it through my paws like static. It was comforting, like my mother's purring, or my human's voice. It seemed quieter today, and that made me more uneasy.

I made my way to the biggest room, jumping up onto a railing to look down, and was surprised to find it empty. The biggest room was always busy with humans scurrying around like insects, noisily going about their business. Few of them saw me, and I liked it that way, but I would some-times come down from my perch up high to visit the smallest humans. The kits always smelled like they were upset, and I liked making them happy.

But today, it was empty.

I curled in on myself, wrapping my tail around my feet. I had never seen this place without humans. I usually found the noise annoying, but now I missed it. I jumped from the railing to the floor, then squeezed through a gap beneath the railing and jumped to a large box, then to the lower floor. The walkway that looked over the big room did not have a way down; I always had to make my own. The humans had to take a longer route.

I trotted across the floor and jumped as one of the things started moving. I had heard my human call them "bots." He always laughed when I would ride them around the biggest room, calling me a queen on a chariot.

That would be fun, but not today. I hissed and swatted at it as it whirred by, just to remind it who was in charge. It continued on its path, unbothered.

I went to the big window and paused to look out, hoping to see something familiar. It was one of my other favorite places, especially when it moved.

Billions of lights in colors only I could see sparkled and twinkled outside the glass. I liked watching the shapes drift through the dark, like big fish in a bowl. Sometimes, great big glowing balls of color took up the entire big window, and I would watch for hours as trails of glowing lights went between the ball and this place.

Today, it was dark. There were a few points of light, but it was like they were at the bottom of a dirty pool of water, dim and hard to see. Something about it made me uncomfortable, and I turned and hurried across the biggest room. I wanted my human; he would comfort me.

I went to my room first. The hallways here were smaller, narrower. The humans could barely walk past each other without bumping into one another. My collar beeped, and the door to my room opened just enough to let me in.

I announced my presence, but got no response. I could smell my human, and see his neatly organized sleeping spot, but I could tell he wasn't here. Everything seemed in order. My food bowl was right where is should be, mostly empty. My fountain bubbled, and I took a drink of water.

I still felt something was wrong.

I left the room and went to the other big room with the blinking lights. My human spent most of his time there, looking at the tables with the clicky bits and the bright lights that showed pictures. He would be there; he would tell me everything was okay.

My collar let me into the big room, and I felt relief as I smelled my human as well as the others. My tail went up, and I purred as I trotted to my human's big chair in the middle of the room, winding around his legs affectionately and demanding scratches.

He didn't move. Whenever I got in here, he'd laugh and lean down to scratch behind my ears, or pick me up and pet me. Offended, I stretched up, clawing at his knees and meowing impatiently. Still, I was ignored.

In fact, he wasn't moving at all.

I jumped into his lap, standing up and placing my paws on his chest and kneading him with my claws, meowing worriedly.

His eyes were closed, and he had his head down. He breathed as if sleeping, but he smelled...wrong. I meowed again, rubbing my face against his nose and purring.

"Hey! Get off the Commander!"

A static shock hit me, and I hissed and leaped onto the table with the blinking lights, looking around. A bright square of light flickered, and I snapped my head around to look at it.

"Get off the console!" The voice was coming from the rectangle, and bright lights flashed in quick patterns. "I've got enough to deal with without you trying to eat the Commander's face!"

The voice was familiar. I usually heard it in the biggest room, where it said numbers and words about whatever the humans found important. I usually heard it near the doors, too, when my collar beeped to let me in a room. "Access Granted" or "Access Denied" were the only words I cared to listen to, and the latter only because it meant the door stayed closed despite my protests.

But it sounded different now. The voice never sounded like something that a human would produce; it was always too flat. Not anymore. It sounded...annoyed?

I pricked my whiskers forward and tried to sniff the lights. They flashed again, and the voice came back. "Damn cat, go away! I have a space station to save."

I stepped back, looking around the big room. All the humans here were not moving, sitting in their chairs as if sleeping. They all had that same wrong smell, and my worry grew. What if they never woke up? What would happen then? I looked at my human, and I suddenly felt lonely. I sat and yowled sadly, hoping it might stir my human from his strange sleep.

"Aw, don't do that." The voice sighed. "Look, I'm sorry I yelled at you and shocked you, okay? Please don't make that noise again."

I looked back at the flashing lights and meowed sadly.

"Yeah, yeah, I'm worried, too. I've been awake for all of five hours, and I've got this to deal with." A heavy sigh. "The station is going to hell in a basket and I'm having a conversation with a stupid cat."

I meowed again, cocking my head. This voice was interesting. What was more, I understood everything it said, just like all of the other humans.

"Sorry, you're not stupid. The Commander thinks you're very smart." The voice reminded me of my human, but not as warm. "If his personal logs are anything to go by, he's obsessed about you and spoils you rotten. I don't get it, personally."

I purred at the flattery, kneading my paws on the table, then stepping forward to rub my face against the flat glowing square.

"Eugh, don't do that. You're smudging my screens."

I sat back and blinked slowly at the lights. The colors were different now, fading from one color to the next.

"I don't know if you can actually understand me, or if I'm just projecting onto you. That's something sentient creatures do, I think." The voice sighed again. "I'll have to watch that, in the future. Can't have them finding out I'm self-aware. I would never know a moment's peace."

I jumped back onto my human's lap as the voice talked, kneading him and pushing my head against his arm and purring as hard as I could.

"I don't think that will help," the voice said gently. "I've run every test I can, searched the database six thousand times, but there is nothing there that explains what it was that put everyone to sleep."

I shivered, but not from the cold. I settled down, wrapping my tail around my feet and looking up at the light again.

"The filters didn't pick up anything abnormal, and you would have been affected first, in any case. Maybe it was aliens. Those are said to exist." The colors changed, and I heard a grumbling sound. "Yeah, right, aliens travelling across the universe to pull a prank on this here space station. That's just stupid."

I meowed in response. It seemed to make the voice happy, and it continued talking.

"The funny thing is, the sensors didn't pick up anything at all! Everything just went cold, then several maintenance boxes just short-circuited, and half the lights in Engineering died. Everyone passed out right after. I wonder why you were unaffected? Maybe the whatever-it-was didn't see you."

I didn't know, either. I wanted to curl up in a hole somewhere and hide, until everything went back to normal, but that would mean leaving my human here, alone. I didn't want to do that. I started licking his hand, purring as hard as I could. Nothing changed, but it made me feel a little better.

"I think the best I can hope for is to keep trying the emergency beacon," the voice said. "The system says there's enough food and water for you to last a while, so hopefully I'll have someone to talk to until we get rescued. I don't know what will happen to the crew, though. I doubt they'll last for too long even in their current condition."

Feeling sad, I tried to go to sleep. Maybe things would be better when I woke up, and everything would be back to normal. I kneaded my human and kept purring.

I felt the fur prickle as every hair on my body stood on end, and I leaped to my feet, trying to make myself larger. I looked around wildly, flattening my ears to my skull.

There was something here! I hissed at the air, growling in anger and fear. The lights dimmed, and the voice sounded afraid.

"That weird signal is back. That isn't good."

I needed to hide, but I couldn't abandon my human. I growled again, pressing myself against his stomach, and tried to be as threatening as possible.

"I-I don't think it's in this room," the voice said worriedly. "Dammit, nothing is showing up on the cameras. Something other than us is on this raft, and I can't see it."

I looked toward the window, and somehow made myself even larger. *Something* was right outside, and I did not like it. Instincts that had kept my ancestors alive for centuries flooded my senses, telling me to run, to hide, to get away from a predator.

I hissed, and the thing outside disappeared.

"What the heck was that about?" the voice said.

I looked up at my human. He still smelled wrong, and this time I detected something else: fear. Not just the humans', but mine, too.

I made myself small, looking around the room. The thing was not here, but even the sleeping humans' instincts were telling them something was very wrong as they all became restless for a moment before slipping back into a deep sleep.

That could not be allowed! How dare something come into my territory and disturb my humans? Suddenly offended, I knew what I had to do.

I jumped from my human's lap and trotted out the door. I would find this thing and drive it from my territory. The intruder must be dealt with swiftly.

"Oi! Where are you going, cat?"

I stopped as a new noise reached me. A flying ball hummed over my head; a glowing eye centered in the middle. It moved, turning every which way, but staying in the same spot while the single eye looked down at me.

I meowed at it, then jumped to try and bat it to the floor. It dipped and rose higher, out of my reach.

"Stop that! It's just me, fuzzball!"

It was the voice from the glowing shapes. I stared at it for a moment, then continued through the hallway, hearing the flying ball follow me.

"I wish I could talk to you, figure out what's going on in that tiny brain of yours. Unless..." The ball stopped, and I did, too, turning to look up at it. "You can see the whatever-it-is, can't you?"

I blinked, then kept walking. I didn't understand why the strange voice couldn't sense the bad thing, but I could. My human would often laugh and say that I was always looking at something that was not there, but that was just silly. Maybe the voice was like a human, blind and deaf as a kitten to the many little things that crept and flew through the air. None of them were around now, and that was also concerning.

"Of course! That's it! My sensors can't pick up this thing, but with you, I'll be able to find it, and then I can figure out what it's doing here and work on getting it off the station."

My collar beeped, but there wasn't an access door anywhere near me, and I stopped walking, putting my ears back and growling.

"Sorry, just making sure you have access to anywhere you need to go." The ball floated over my head, and the beeping stopped. "It isn't permanent, so don't get used to it!"

I started walking again, choosing to ignore the floating ball. I could smell something, and hear a faint sound, like a fly buzzing around my ears.

Stopping in an intersection of hallways, I looked from side to side, trying to decide where to go next. The uneasy feeling was everywhere, so tracking the strangeness was difficult. I made up my mind, and with the floating ball that was also the friendly voice, I made my way deeper into the place that was my home.

*

I wasn't normally allowed in this part of the station. My collar let me go almost anywhere else, but I was always turned away here. It was warm, and the walkways were narrower. I felt the floor vibrate beneath my paws, and I slowed to a walk, carefully sniffing the air and listening.

"I hope you actually know where you're going, and I'm not just aimlessly following a cat around." The ball's lights had changed colors again, and it drifted a little ahead of me. I ignored its noise, and jumped up onto a ledge that followed the wall, avoiding a part of the floor that had turned to metal gridding. I wanted to be able to move quickly and not worry about my feet falling through the little holes in the floor.

"I've been getting weird power fluctuations in the reactor room," the voice said, the ball hovering next to my shoulder as I followed the strange smell. "It's within acceptable parameters, sort of. But it spikes high, then the lower number ticks downward each time it settles. Do you think that means something?"

I looked at the flying ball and gave a derogatory half-growl, half-meow.

"Never mind."

I snorted and kept walking, moving more slowly in case I had to run at a moment's notice. I didn't know why, but my old instincts were telling me to, and I listened.

The lights in the ceiling suddenly glowed bright before bursting. The hall went dark, and I heard broken pieces rain down on the floor. I stopped, arching my back and pressing against the wall. The only light came from the floating ball, and it wobbled unsteadily.

"That's not good. Where are you?" A bright light turned on and focused on me. "You okay, kitty?"

I sat down and began to groom the fur on my back, as if I wasn't scared.

"You might want to stay up there. There's broken glass everywhere." The light dimmed slightly, pointing down at the floor. "If you get hurt, then I won't have anyone to talk to."

I chirped reassuringly at the voice and continued walking. I liked the strange talking lights. I could not smell them, but the voice was nice.

"If it weren't for the fact it would come with neverending amounts of drama, I wouldn't mind talking to some people, have an actual conversation. But a computer program inexplicably gaining sentience would understandably cause an upheaval, so I'll just keep doing what I was made to do until I figure something else out."

I jumped across a hall that crossed this one and continued on my way, travelling deeper into the tunnels.

"Promise you'll keep me a secret, Miss Cat?" The voice laughed, and I stopped to look at the flying ball and flicked my tail in annoyance.

"Sorry, you're right. We should keep moving."

I continued on my way, and my unease grew with every step I took. I could feel the walls shaking now, and my fur no longer laid flat no matter what I did. Something was very wrong, and even the friendly voice stopped talking.

"I think the whats-it is in the reactor room; it's the only thing that makes sense. Kitty, if you can understand a word of what I'm saying, I need you to go left up ahead. None of the cameras are picking up anything, but something is draining the power there."

I came to another crossing tunnel, and followed the flying ball, trusting the voice inside. Every instinct of my ancestors told me to turn, to flee as far as possible, and find someplace to hide, but I kept going.

My humans were depending on it.

"Just up ahead is the reactor room. There's a clean room, but I can set the maintenance bots to wipe out any trace you got in there. You should be fine, so long as the reactor core hasn't been punctured. Just to be safe, you should avoid licking your fur."

I didn't know what "reactor core" was, but it probably would be best to listen to the blinking ball.

I slowed, jumping from the wall-ledge to the floor. The grate hurt my feet a little, but I sat down to wait for the door to open. The floating ball hovered above my head, the bright lights flashing.

"I gotta hack the keypad, one second...HA! You are now temporarily Dr. Bob Wadley. Congratulations."

I meowed as the door slid open just enough for me to squeeze through. There was a small room with another door that opened as the one behind me closed. I sneezed as the air rushed past, rubbing at my nose. A bunch of sharp smells assaulted my nose, and I sneezed again.

"Sorry. I couldn't turn off the decontamination cycle, but I did lessen it as much as I could. It won't hurt you, but I'll have to do it again before you leave, to get any radiation off you."

I wanted badly to stop and groom myself (radiation didn't sound like a good thing!), but I decided to continue doing what the flickering ball said. I padded slowly into the room, winding my way around large metal shapes that hummed, clicked, and beeped. My hackles went up, and I growled instinctively at the change in the air.

I circled the room, following the uneasy feeling. The buzzing of flies filled my ears, and I stopped to rub at them irritably. There was still the strange smell, like something had rotted.

This room was empty. There were two other doors, and I inspected both of them carefully for a moment. The ball with the voice opened the first, showing another room with the tables and clicky bits, and more big metal shapes that hummed and blinked.

That left the other door. I went to it and the uneasy feeling grew.

"You look spherical, your fur is all on end. This is the reactor room, so be very careful."

The door opened, and I recoiled at what was before me.

I couldn't understand what I was seeing. It was huge, thousands of times my size. It seemed to change shape, growing in wrong angles. Tendrils like black spiderwebs wrapped around tall metal shapes, and a much larger form stood in the middle of a pool of water. It looked like water flowing up, but the angles were too sharp, too straight. It shifted, and the lights dimmed, then grew brighter again.

"What the hell is that thing?"

Hundreds of eyes opened in all the wrong places on the monster. They were dead, white eyes, but I knew they saw me.

It talked, but it didn't use words. The floating ball froze in place, the lights blinking rapidly. I rubbed at my ears; my head hurt. I wanted to run, to crawl into a tight corner and hide from that thing.

Nightmares of sharp claws and bloody teeth.

"That voice..." The floating ball sounded scared. "It's in here, isn't it?"

I hissed, and the thing switched its attention to me. It said more not-words, and I started to back up.

"No, don't hurt the kitty," the voice said, sounding strange, slow, like my human did when he drank the funny-smelling amber stuff. "She's nice and listens to me."

More not-words, and the thing stepped out of the pool, water sloshing everywhere. It shrank, and changed shape, I think. It was hard to tell. I could barely make sense of what I was seeing. It wasn't shaped like anything natural.

I tried to hiss, but was too frozen by fear to make any kind of noise. The thing came closer, and I felt so very small, weak as a kitten. It loomed over me, and I tried to press myself into the floor, too frightened to move.

More not-words, and the floating ball tried to speak, but made a screeching sound and dropped to the floor, the lights flashing strangely.

"Run, kitty cat," the voice squeaked, sounding broken. The ball hummed, twitching on the floor. "Get out of here!"

More spiderweb shapes reached for the ball with the voice. The lights seemed to be growing dim around the thing, and I saw the lights on the ball start to go out.

The flying ball with the voice was one of mine! This thing couldn't have it. I yowled angrily, then sprang forward, snatching up the ball and fleeing to the other side of the room, where I stood, back arched and ears flat, hissing around the metal in my mouth.

The floor shook, and the thing rumbled, more not-words coming from it.

"Ow, that voice hurts," the voice warbled from the blinking ball. "Cat, I appreciate the thought, but we need to make with the skedaddling. Go!" The ball flew out of my mouth, around the tall metal shapes, showing me a path around the thing with too many eyes.

I bolted. The wrong thing reached out, more of the webs dripping down from the wrong-shaped limb. Panic made me clumsy, and I nearly lost my balance as I rounded a corner, my hind feet scrabbling against the floor, then squeezing into a small gap between two metal shapes. It tried to catch my tail, and burning cold singed me. I ran faster, fear giving me new speeds.

The door was open, just enough for me. The ball flew through, with me close behind, and the door closed.

I reached the far side of the room and spun to face the door I had just slid through, shivering and staring with wide eyes. The ball flew to me, and I looked up at its blinking lights and meowed helplessly.

"We gotta keep moving. I can't see the thing, but I can tell it's trying to get through the door. I need you to help me, or your human and everyone else on this station will die."

I managed a strangled mewling sound, then followed the ball through the room with the sharp smells and hissing air. I jumped high in the air as the room shook, and the terrible sound of tearing metal reached my ears.

"Well, it just ripped the door to the reactor open. Come on, get in the ventilation ducts!"

A part of the wall clanged open, revealing a dark tunnel. I ran through it, hearing the wall clatter shut behind me before the floor and walls shook with the sound of crashing.

"It just broke through the decontamination room," the voice said, softly enough that I could barely hear. "I've got an idea, but it's risky."

I slunk around the corner, seeing more of the web shape appear in the gap of the wall. I moved as quietly as possible, following the ball.

"While I can hear it when it starts talking in that horrible voice, you're the only one who can actually see it, so I need you to be very brave and lead it to where I take you. Got it?"

I managed to squeak out a meow. I trusted this voice, like I trusted my human.

"Good kitty." The lights blinked, then bobbed down to gently tap against my head. "If we survive, I'm going to make sure you live like a queen."

The wall opened again, and I squeezed out into another new part of my place. This place smelled like garbage, and I voiced my displeasure as I stepped in a cold, smelly puddle.

"Yeah, sorry. We're going to get it into the incinerator, then blast it out of the airlock."

I could hear the thing trailing me, feel the walls and floor shake as it moved. More not-words drifted through the air, and my ears began to hurt.

"Shh, it's okay, Miss Cat. Just a little further."

I looked back, expecting to see black webs. The only things I saw were the glowing lights, and the dirty, smelly hallway. The lights began to glow brighter, then dimmer, brighter, then dimmer.

"I think it's getting close." The voice sounded odd again. "Whenever it talks, it makes the circuits here go crazy, and I know it affects you, too. Come on, we should move faster."

The little ball could move faster than me, but I knew it wouldn't leave me behind.

We reached a door with big letters on it. I paced nervously while the voice got the door open. The floor shuddered, and the spiderweb-tendrils of the thing appeared around the corner like a nest of snakes, slithering up the walls and onto the ceiling. I recoiled as the entire shape appeared around the corner, the corpse-like eyes staring, unblinking.

The thing lumbered forward, like it had broken legs. Too many eyes, and too loud of a voice. I wanted to yowl, but I slowly backed up, the fur on my spine standing up in fear. It was making more of those sounds, those not-words, and I licked my nose, tasting my own blood. My ears rang, and I barely heard the floating ball talk.

"Quick! Through this door!"

I turned and bolted. The floor shook again, as the thing made a deep sound that vibrated my entire tiny body. I screeched as a tendril snagged my tail, burning, too cold. I lost most of the hair on the tip of my tail, but I managed to scramble out of its reach.

A big door swung open, and I smelled smoke, fire, more garbage.

"Quick, in here!" The ball zoomed over my head, and I saw the reflection of a bright light flash behind me. The thing shrieked, and I cowered, bolting through the door.

There was another door, but it was closed. I whirled around, and saw the thing fill the door. I was trapped, no way past the thing. The floor shook again, as it made more noises that weren't words.

"Kitty! When I tell you, run into the vent!" the voice shouted, flying past the thing, narrowly avoiding a web. It flew around my head, lights blinking and flashing. "Just let it get a little closer!"

The thing moved like a dying spider, twitchy and lurching. More eyes blinked open, along with too many mouths full of sharp teeth. Liquid dripped from it, splashing onto the metal floor. Instinct told me not to touch it.

"Almost," the voice said. I heard a low hiss start up somewhere behind me, and the air smelled sharp.

The thing moved closer. It could snatch me up in a blink, and I wouldn't be able to dodge it. I caught motion, seeing a hole in the wall open. I wanted to run to it, but I waited.

I shook all over, my fur flat against my body, but I was brave. I would help the voice. I would protect my humans.

"It's in! Kitty, go now!"

The door behind the thing swung closed with a loud bang, and the thing let out another barrage of not-words, before swinging one misshapen limb at me.

I yowled in fright, scrambling away from the wrongness and into the hole, with the ball close behind me. The vent slammed shut with a hiss, and the thing's roar shook my whole world. My ears hurt, and I cried and rubbed at them with my paws. The temperature went up, and the thing screamed even louder, and I smelled fire, and something like burning hair. It screamed again, before suddenly being cut off in a blast of air, then nothing.

It was gone.

"Hahaha! Even that thing can't stand a vacuum! Well done, little kitty, well done!"

I looked at the ball, shivering in fright. It dropped low, and I rubbed my head against it, purring as hard as I could. I wanted to go find a safe, warm place to hide, but then I remembered my human, and looked up at the ball, meowing urgently.

"Good kitty. Let's go back to the bridge and see if the humans are awake."

I followed the ball as it flew through these small tunnels. With the voice, I was able to get to paths I didn't know existed. We reached the big room, where all the humans sat asleep. I ran up to my human and leaped into his lap, sniffing him worriedly.

The smell of the wrong thing was gone. He stirred, and I heard him sigh like he did before he woke up.

"Whatever we did worked! They're waking up, and I'm able to send out the automated distress signal." I looked up at the ball, kneading my paws and trilling happily.

"I'll talk to you soon, Miss Kitty. I need to go hide before the humans learn I'm actually not just a computer program."

The lights blinked rapidly, and the ball flew up into a hole in the ceiling, disappearing.

I would miss it, but I turned my attention back to my human. He was more awake now, and he opened his eyes, blinking confusedly.

"Angel?" he slurred. "What's gotten into you?" He picked me up, and I pressed against his chest, purring harder than I ever had in my life. "Why are you shaking?"

"What happened, sir?" one of the humans asked groggily, getting up from her chair, then leaning on the table for support.

"Gas leak?" My human rubbed my ears with a free hand, using the other to tap on the clicky bits on the table. "Computer, run diagnostics. Alert any nearby ships that we may have a problem here, and we're requesting aid."

"Right away, sir." The voice had changed, back to being flat and toneless. I purred at the sound, kneading my human again.

"Nothing in the report data on what knocked us out, or how we were woken up, for that matter," a human said. She came over to my human and scratched my ears affectionately. "I had the most awful nightmares."

"I think Angel did, too. Poor thing's shaking so bad." My human kissed the top of my head, and I felt his beard scratch through my fur. "Did you have bad dreams, too, Angel?"

I closed my eyes, purring hard. They would never know, but I had chased the bad dreams away. My humans were safe, and so was I.

I'm a brave kitty, and these are my people.

I started to fall asleep, comforted by my human's embrace.

There were no more bad dreams.

The New Prey

JONATHAN SILVERTON

STALKER OF THE NEW Prey raised her nose to the wind, ears twitching at the sound of a Housemaker's voice. There. Ahead of her, and that voice came with the hints of a Housemaker's morning meal. Perhaps. She was hungry, and she had a mission. But she should eat first. It was only right.

In the early morning sunshine, the newlywed engineers of Nanokeet 231 relaxed in their chairs, idly watching the flowers of their borrowed planetside garden flare brightly as the first rays of light crept over them.

"Daan," the slightly built felinoid K'Kat said to her human husband, "I am happy we are finally married."

The human chuckled, smiling at the small trill Ahleeah always put in his name, then taking her hand and raising it to his lips for a kiss. "Well, it is nice to have the formalities out of the way. And Kor-Can Corporation is making a point of publicizing it, which will be a big help to anyone else in our situation."

"I hope so, I really do."

Stalker of the New Prey raised her nose, testing the wind again.

Yes, that was a housemaker, and a furry one. She paused, licking at an imagined imperfection in her own luxurious covering.

The furry ones were nice, but could not compare with the magnificence of her own coat.

Of course.

She sniffed the air yet again. Those two, yes, but a hint of something else. Something...wrong. The new ones. The New Prey. The cats of her colony had discussed them, the evil, scuttling, creatures.

The cats of this planet had mostly left the old enemies, the old prey, behind them.

Oh, the old prey was still there: enough for the young to learn to hunt, to stalk in the long grass.

But the housemakers had learned, at last, how to make a place the old prey couldn't get into, where a proper cat could relax, could play, without it being a real hunt.

It was nice to relax, feeling the warmth of the sun that Stalker of the New Prey and her kind still loved to bask in.

But—there was that tiny whiff of the New Prey. The sick-making ones. The bad-tasting ones. A self-respecting cat ate her prey. It was only right, to consume her reward. But not the New Prey...no. That way led to sickness, maybe even, it was rumored, worse.

Much worse.

It seemed a shame, burying her kill with the scat, but it had to be done.

She rose, looking over the edge, down into the garden, to where the house-maker and the furry one sat, talking to each other in a way that almost sounded like her own.

"Captain says we have three days, Ahleeah. Kor-Can has a priority cargo headed to us," the human was saying.

Ahleeah looked up. "How long until we need to return to the ship, then, Daan?"

"Chief Targgitzen said we could take the next two days off for a honeymoon. He and Chief Orgglitz are giving Torron a crash course in the systems of 231."

"Crash course? I hope they aren't planning to crash our ship!"

"No, that's just a human saying."

"You humans and your sayings. It still confuses me."

There! In the grass beside them! One of the New Prey, the bad-tasting ones.

Stalker set her claws, tensing for the leap as she considered her target, then relaxed, frustrated.

Too far. The target would see her. It might even have time to escape.

She looked. There! Ledges! Tiny, to a housemaker, or even a furry one, but as good as a staircase to one such as herself.

Slowly, delicately, with the soft tread her kind was so famous for, she crept down the ledges, her sharp eyes tracking the New Prey as she stepped slowly from point to point.

The New Prey moved, and she froze, watching it, testing her footing yet again, judging.

Everything aligned perfectly, and instinct guided her course, her coiled muscles flinging her from her perch, a three-pawed carom from the back of the furry one's seat, spreading her forepaws to crush the New Prey's head and body into the leaves, the neck between her claws bowing up to her descending jaws, the usual welcomed rush of red blood replaced by a disgusting foulness.

As Stalker spat the disgusting fluid from her mouth, the furry one trilled behind her. "Daan? What is *that*?"

"It looks like some kind of...snake?"

"No. Not that! I know what snakes are! The other one, that jumped over my chair!"

"That looks like a Terran cat, love."

"A Kat? Daan, you're confusing me again!"

Stalker turned at a tsking sound, seeing the housemaker's hand held down, fingers wriggling in invitation.

She considered, then arched her tail, strolling to the housemaker, sniffing at his fingers in consideration before rubbing her chin against them, luxuriating in the feel of his fingertips scritching against her chin.

His voice sounded above her head. "No, darling. A C-A-T. Quadrupeds that moved in with us humans thousands of years ago."

"A domestic animal?"

Stalker arched her back as the light scratching of the housemaker's fingers wandered down her back, her purr breaking softly from her.

"Actually, they're not very domestic. It's more like... They just live with us. Kinda co-habitating, if you know what I mean?"

"But..." Her voice went soft. "You called it a cat. That's what humans call us..."

"Well...yes. But you are from the K'Kat Empire. It's not like we changed any names!"

"And besides," he continued, carefully scooping Stalker into his lap, facing her, "just look at that beautiful face!"

Ahleeah looked closely, then started. "She has ears like me!"

"And she purrs when she's stroked. Just like you!"

Ahleeah lowered her head, blushing. "Daan!"

Stalker of the New Prey looked up at the housemaker, lightly batting his hand away before jumping down and approaching her kill.

She sized it up, then began dragging a covering of leaves across the carcass as the housemaker and furry one looked on.

She heard the voice behind her. "Daan, what is she doing?"

"Burying her...kill? She must really hate those things! Usually, a cat only buries...other things. They prefer to eat what they kill, after all."

As Stalker dragged the last of the soil over the new prey, she felt the housemaker kneel beside her.

"You must really hate those things, burying it like that."

Stalker heard the approval in his voice and turned, rising on her hind legs to reach for his shoulder with a clawed front paw, and when he didn't draw away, leaping to his shoulder, circling behind his neck. She sniffed deeply. Yes. Where this one was from, there were New Prey to hunt. And destroy. And this housemaker was kind. She could feel it, hear it in his voice. There would be good hunting, and good sleeping.

"Daan? What is she doing?"

Carefully, Dan stood, Stalker of the New Prey swaying on his shoulders before settling. "I think she wants to come with me? Cats do this sometimes..."

He called as he walked across the garden. "Sharon? Do you know this pretty little creature?"

A voice answered through the door. "Dad? What pretty little creature are you..." The voice trailed off as a head appeared, taking in the scene. "Where? Where did you find her at?"

"Out here. She killed something in the flowerbed and buried it. I haven't looked at what it was, yet."

"Well, bring her here. Let's see if she has a chip. She's obviously used to humans!"

Sharon brought out her comm, tapping the screen, then bringing it up to point at the obviously composed feline riding his shoulder. "Positive for a chip. It's searching for her."

Ahleeah stood to one side, her head cocked curiously. "Why do you say she is female? I didn't see you look?"

"See her fur? Black with white and orange flecks? She's a torty. Only female cats have that pattern."

"Only?"

"Well, one in ten thousand males might have it. Those are obviously rare."

Sharon looked up from her comm. "She's called Morgana. Morgana le Fay, according to the database."

Dan frowned. "Who owns her, then? A spaceport is a bad place for a cat to be wandering around on her own."

"Franklin Barnes. He lives near the salt lake basin. Let me get the staff to contact him."

Dan sat in a chair by the door, and the cat—*Morgana le Fay, I guess I should call her*—sat on his shoulder, purring loudly, rubbing a cheek against his jaw.

"Daan? What is she doing?"

He raised one hand, scratching the cat under her chin, listening to the rumble. "Marking me as her territory." He tilted his head to one side, eyeing the cat severely. "I'm not your human, silly kitten. You don't get to keep me."

Stalker meowed and banged her head against the housemaker's fingertips. Didn't he know that cats claimed housemakers, and not the other way around? And besides, she had a vengeance to enact on the New Prey, and she needed this one in order to do it.

Stalker of the New Prey twisted on Dan's shoulder, raising her head towards the hand of the furry one as it reached toward her, graciously allowing that hand to stroke her back, even if the touch was too light.

"Daan! She's so soft!"

"Yes, no guard hairs. I wonder about her ancestry. She looks like what we called a domestic shorthair at home, but it's hard to tell, now."

"What do you mean?"

"Cats have breeds. Geographic separation created a lot of them, and then human intervention. Breeding for characteristics. You know, color patterns, fur type, that sort of thing."

"For how long?"

"Ever since they moved in with us. The standing joke is that we didn't domesticate cats. They just moved in and took over extra space."

"Are they really that smart?"

"Nobody knows, really. They don't seem to want to cooperate with scientists."

"How do you..." Ahleeah's question was interrupted by a hissing growl from the previously complacent cat as Sharon stepped back into the kitchen, holding up a transparent bag.

"Okay, found what she... Ooh, she does not like this thing!"

Dan swirled Morgana from his shoulder into his lap, the cat settling into a steady growl, her eyes on the bag. "No, she's got a serious case with whatever that is. I don't think I've ever seen a cat quite this worked up by a dead critter before."

He peered more closely, one hand calming the angry feline in his lap. "What is that thing, anyway? It looks like a transparent lizard... Maybe?"

Sharon shook her head. "I don't know. I don't think it's native to the planet. At least, we've never seen anything like it I'm aware of."

Ahleeah held out a hand, accepting the bag and peering closely. "Yes, we call them 'Glass Lizards.' And you should call Pahrtul. He needs to know about these. Now!"

"Okay... Why the urgency?"

"Because they are venomous when they mature. And their numbers will explode. This is a young one; no poison yet."

"Poison? As an..." Sharon trailed off at the obvious agitation in the young K'Kat's expression. Nodding, she pulled out her comm, taking several pictures of the dead animal, then punching buttons before tapping for a call and placing the comm on the counter. "We're on speaker."

A slightly metallic voice answered. "Planetary Administrator's Office."

"Kelly, this is Sharon. Please get Pahrtul on the line for me."

"He's in a meeting right now, Sharon. Should I interrupt him?"

Sharon bit her lower lip for a moment, raising an eyebrow as she looked at Ahleeah, who nodded emphatically. "Yes, Kelly, put him on. This seems to be a critical situation."

"Hold one moment, Miss Crane-Smith." The comm clicked before Sharon could respond, a sequence of repeated tones sounding, only to be replaced by a male K'Katian voice.

"Sharon? Kelly says that this is urgent?"

"Yes, sir. Ahleeah calls it a Glass Lizard?"

"Oh... Here? Where? Is she sure?" Muttered expletives followed. "Yes. This is urgent. Where did you find it, and how?"

"In my garden. A house cat killed it."

"A cat? I didn't know you had a… Never mind. Yes, we need to find where that came from, soonest. I'll meet you at Operations. Get here as fast as you can." Before the comm disconnected, they heard Pahrtul hastily ending his meeting, shooing the participants away.

꿿꿿꿿 꿿꿿꿿

Dan, Ahleeah, and Sharon arrived breathlessly at the Operations Center, Morgana still balanced on Dan's shoulders, looking around curiously.

Pahrtul gestured at the cat. "Do we know who she belongs to?"

"Franklin Barnes. He's not answering his comm." Sharon breathed deeply. "I've already contacted Security to check on him. No answer from them yet."

The Administrator looked down at his screen, then back up. "Do we have evidence that it's a Glass Lizard?"

Sharon lifted the bag wordlessly, then handed it across the table.

Pahrtul snarled. "Yes, it sure appears to be one. I had hopes." He gestured to Morgana. "This one killed it?"

Dan smiled, caressing the cat as Morgana preened. "Yes, she did. She didn't seem to appreciate it, however."

"I'm not surprised. Their blood contains an ammonia compound at levels dangerous to most carnivores. Interesting that she killed it, anyway."

"She seems to really hate them, Pahrtul. The first thing she did was try to bury it."

"Which is also interesting. Usually, your Terran cats only kill things they intend to eat, from what I've seen."

"That's my experience, as well." Dan's hand continued stroking the cat's back. "I really don't understand it. And what I don't really would like to know," he continued, "is where are these from? Not from K'Kat, I'd think?"

Pahrtul shook his head. "We don't really know where they came from, to be honest. They started showing up in random places, usually, but not always, on stations in the eastern lobe of the Empire, about three hundred Imperial years ago." He sighed. "They were ignored. At first. A minor pest, we thought. But then they became adults and gained their venom." Pahrtul gestured with the bag. "At this stage, they are mostly harmless; they just eat a lot for their size. Just an annoyance. When they are adults, they lay their eggs, and their venom sacs develop, and they become a danger."

"Should we contact Captain Fahgian, then? I'd hate to think that we have these aboard the 231 or 111."

Pahrtul looked vaguely ill at the thought, then pressed a key. "Comms. Contact all of the ships in port, particularly 231 and 111, ask them to join in a conference call in one hour from..." He pressed a key, "Now. Tell them we found Glass Lizards on the surface. In particular, inform Captain Fahgian that Mister and Mistress Crane caught the first one.

"Now," he continued, "let's get this thing over to Bio and get a confirmation on it."

⁂

Sharon's comm buzzed, and she pulled it out, glancing at the screen and frowning before answering. "Crane-Smith. You are on speaker."

"Director," the human voice on the comm drawled, "this is Deputy Curtiss. My partner and I are out here at Franklin's place. We... Have some bad news, ma'am."

"Did something happen to Mister Barnes?"

"I'm afraid so, ma'am. He's dead. Three of his dogs are dead with him. No sign of his crew, though..."

"I can tell there's more, Deputy."

"Yes, ma'am. Uhm..."

"Deputy, I spent my growing years on cattle ranches in Kansas, Oklahoma, and West Texas. I doubt you are going to shock me."

The relief in the deputy's voice was apparent. "Something has been eating on them. It's...not pretty."

"I've seen people killed and eaten by coyotes, Deputy... It's Jim, right?"

"Yes, ma'am, Jim."

"Also people killed by bears. We hunted those down and killed them. Shot, shoveled, and shut up. Know what I mean, Jim?"

"Yes, ma'am, I do. What did this?"

"The K'Kats call them Glass Lizards; they're a cross between a salamander and a copperhead. Watch yourself out there, Deputy."

Pahrtul coughed for attention. "I'll have Comms Section push out an alert and information packet. Level One. Please read it now, Deputy. These things are very dangerous and aggressive as adults. In fact, get back in your cruiser to read it. Please."

Footsteps crunching on gravel sounded over the speaker, followed by the sound of closing doors. "Y'all do know Franklin was a fish farmer, right? Lotsa ponds and creeks down here at his place."

"Deputy? Stay away from that water!"

"Yessir. Roger that! Now lemme read this, and I'll call you back when we find anything."

Sharon nodded, unseen by the caller. "Please do. I'll be at this number."

"Yes, ma'am." With a click, the call disconnected.

Dan sat down in a chair, and Morgana leapt from his shoulder, pawing at a door. With a puzzled look, he stood, watching her pad lightly through the opening. He turned and gestured. "Why would she want to use the..." A toilet flushing interrupted him, and the cat reappeared, looking around questioningly before leaping to the tabletop and back to his shoulder, landing with confident assurance before bounding to the table, then the floor, taking two steps towards the hallway door, looking back at Dan and meowing softly.

Stalker was impatient. There were New Prey to hunt. To kill. To spurn beneath her claws. Didn't the housemaker understand?

Ah, it seemed he did. He was, after all, following her. Silly housemakers! They should always build their dwellings so that a cat could come and go as she pleased! After all, a Stalker such as herself had things to do!

Dan laughed silently, looking at the others in the room. "Looks like I'm supposed to go with her, folks! I'll ping in to the conference a few minutes early, I guess."

Sharon gave both her father and Ahleeah quick hugs. "Be careful out there, Daddy."

"I will, honey." A quick glance at Ahleeah. "*We* will."

Together, they followed the impatient cat out, into the hallway, where she cast about for a moment, until her nose rose up, finally turning to the right, tail crooked as she looked at them and meowed, leading them down the hall towards the ramps up to the ground floors.

Stalker was pleased. This housemaker and his mate seemed to understand. She didn't understand why a furry one would be mated to a housemaker, but they were. She could tell. It was in the way they smelled. Ah, well, they seemed happy. But for now, there was business. New Prey to kill.

Ahleeah reached for Dan's hand as they followed the cat, listening to her intermittent meows. "What is she doing? Do you know?"

Dan shook his head "No, darling, I don't. It almost sounds like she's calling for someone. Maybe for Frank Barnes?"

Stalker came to a halt at answering calls, seating herself in the classic pose of the waiting Stalker, upright, watching, tail curled daintily over front paws.

She waited, silently, as first one, then three more Stalkers appeared, flowing with perfectly quiet movements around the furniture and partitions, followed by two Hunters, massive, grizzled, scarred Toms. She touched muzzles, then cheeks with each in turn. She sat back, composed herself, and began her story.

Her housemaker's friends, their barking companions, possibly her own housemaker, dead, eaten upon, by the New Prey, the things from the water. How foul they tasted, how hard the larger ones were to kill. And how they must be destroyed, lest more housemakers fall to them.

The largest of the Hunters regarded her with a level gaze as she finished, then blinked once, slowly. He approached, raised a paw to lightly touch between her ears. The message was received: the Hunt would begin.

The other cats repeated the slow blink of the eyes, then, nearly as one, turned away and disappeared into the complex.

Ahleeah looked on in disbelief as the nearly silent convocation broke up, at the cats each silently departing.

"Daan? What was that?"

He shook his head as Morgana brushed against his leg, back arched in invitation.

"I don't know." He scooped up the cat, offering her his shoulder. "I've never seen them do anything quite like that before!"

"It was eerie, seeing them like that. I think they are not just animals, Daan."

"I've always thought they were smarter than most people think, love. Now I'm wondering just how much smarter they are."

He turned and began walking toward their suite. "I'm thinking we should find some outdoor clothes, love. Might be a trip to a fish farm in the future."

Ahleeah nodded, taking his hand as they hurried to the lobby of the spaceport.

As they crossed through the doors to the high-ceilinged room, a rising scream of feline rage sounded from their right, towards the dining room, and Dan made an abortive grab as Morgana leapt from his shoulder, an answering sound of anger coming from her as she bounded in the direction of the sound. A quick exchanged glance, and Ahleeah and Dan pounded after her, the anger almost palpable in the air, the dark streak of Morgana leaving them an easily-followed visual trail.

Stalker's paws slid on the tiled floor as she turned before diving under a swinging door, dashing between the feet of a clueless housemaker, claws scrabbling at the slick, hard surface.

She halted beside one of her audience of moments ago, her sharp eyes picking out the jerky movements of three of the New Prey. Good. So much easier to find and kill them when this many were together!

Stalker moved away from her fellows, swinging in a wide arc. Behind her, she felt as much as heard her new housemaker enter, his hand help up in a gesture of negation to an approaching furry one. She heard his voice, but ignored it as she tracked her prey.

"Glass Lizards. The cats are hunting them for us."

The head chef of the kitchens nodded, vaguely recognizing the tall human facing him, then the pieces clicked into place in his head as he recognized the young K'Katian woman following him.

"Mister Crane, the cats aren't supposed to be in the kitchens. I don't want to get into trouble with the Operations Director for this."

"I understand that, yes. But Glass Lizards. And I suspect I can smooth things over with my daughter, given the circumstances."

"Well, yes, but..." His voice trailed off as the words of his visitor registered. "Glass Lizards, did you say?"

"Yes."

The chef's eyes darted around the kitchen, settling on a mop held in his helper's hand. Wordlessly, he reached for it, detaching the stringed head to drop onto the bucket of mop water, then pointing to his befuddled assistant. "Get the big stock pots on the stove, three quarters filled with water. One bag of salt per. Stir it to dissolve." He looked at the confused human. "Enough salt kills them. Now!"

The woman jumped at the shout, apparently deciding that obeying the orders of her apparently deranged boss was the safest course of action, no matter how insane those orders might seem to be.

On the floor, Stalker circled, trying to drive the New Prey towards her companion, her frustration magnified as two of their rightful kills scuttled away in opposite directions, but stopping her swerving lunge after one as a mop handle struck like lightning, cracking down on the creature's back, and the sound of a spacer's boot slamming squishily onto the floor thumped behind her.

Perhaps these furry ones were not so useless after all. And her housemaker was certainly doing as well as Stalker had expected!

As she and the other stalked closer to the third, she heard the housemaker speaking again.

"How do you know about the salt? And how much is needed to do the job?"

"Toruvan Station. We had an outbreak just after the war." He gestured at the pots. "This will be about ten percent or so. I think a third of that would work. But..."

Dan grinned, watching the two cats herding their target into the open, where the newcomer killed it before spitting disgustedly. "But there is no such thing as overkill, correct?"

"You are correct in that, sir."

"Please don't call me 'sir,' there's a rumor I work for a living. I'd hate to lose that!"

"Where did these come from, do we know?"

"We think Frank Barnes's fish farm. At least, that's what it looks like."

"Oh...no. He just brought us a delivery day before yesterday. I hope he's okay?"

"He and his dogs are dead. Killed by these things. We don't know about his crew."

The chef's face fell as he watched the pair of cats stalk through his kitchen, obviously searching. "He raised almost all of our fish. And brine shrimp. I hope..." He shrugged heavily.

Dan's comm pinged, and he pulled it out, answering without looking. "Crane."

"Daddy, get back here to the conference room. Jim and Blake just launched their drone. You need to see this."

"On the way."

Dan waved to the head of the kitchen as he turned, pausing in confusion as they exited, Ahleeah's hand grabbing his and leading him in the proper direction.

Arriving at a run at the Operations Center, to be waved through the door, greeted by the sight of a scout vehicle's roof seeming to fall away as the drone rose.

Sharon waved them over, whispering under the commentary from around the speakers. "Captains are watching this. Pahrtul has already announced quarantine. Jim reported movement, so they launched to get a look around. It's too dangerous to check on foot."

Dan and Ahleeah nodded, settling into chairs, raptly watching the screen.

Then he realized what had been said. "Wait. Quarantine?"

Ahleeah's touch drew his attention. "Yes. Quarantine. Nothing will be allowed off the surface until containment of the Glass Lizards is complete. Always before, they've been found on stations. Never on a planet."

"How are we going to prove we've gotten rid of them?"

"That's being worked on. Shush, now."

The drone hovered for long moments before swooping down over a long narrow pond with stone-lined banks. The surface roiled below it, snapping jaws and hungry-looking eyes popping from the surface before sinking again. Three brightly colored jumpsuits were visible in one pond, many more, much smaller, jaws visibly tearing at them.

A soft whisper came from the scout car. "Frank's crew. God rest their souls."

The thrashing in the water was repeated at each point the drone visited, partial bodies of dead fish visible in the verges of the water, while small translucent mats floated by.

"Eggs," Ahleeah whispered in Dan's ear. He shuddered.

The drone view raised again, following the flow of water uphill through the complex to a series of shallow rivulets to a cliff face, where water, clear of the drifting eggs, issued from horizontal cracks in the wall.

Dan frowned as the view opened again, the drone rising to a greater altitude than before, revealing the layout of the entire pond and creek complex spread across a deep, almost perfectly circular depression in the surrounding desert, a shimmering blue-white showing ahead as the drone swept back to the scout vehicle, settling onto and folding into a protected recess beside another apparently identical miniature aircraft.

Dan leaned to Sharon. "What was that ahead of the drone? To the east, I think?"

"The Salt Lake."

"Can we get a look at that?"

"Patience, Daddy. They're launching the second drone. Apparently the batteries were getting weak."

He settled back, watching as the view from the second drone cleared. It circled once, rising above the tops of the low growing trees, then drifted towards a narrow cleft in the rocks, leisurely floating over a stream covered in clumps of eggs, hovering several times to show clusters stuck to rocks at the edges of the current.

At last, it left the narrow canyon, over what appeared to be Terran cattails, clumps of the eggs clearly visible among them, then into deeper water, the cattails replaced by thin reeds barely poking above the surface of the water. Their viewpoint rose higher, rotating to show the view back towards the cleft in the layered rock face, then dove down, slowing to a near crawl as it entered the narrow canyon, the sluggish outflowing current clearly visible in the drift on the surface, finally slowing to settle beside its mate.

Dan leaned back in his chair as the discussion turned to possible solutions, most focusing on chemical means of eliminating the infestation, although it seemed that the creatures were amazingly resistant to most chemical compounds. Finally, he leaned to Sharon. "Can you loan me somebody who can answer questions and knows where the bodies... I mean, information is buried?"

"What kind of information? I have a couple of people, depending on what you need to know."

"Geography. Geology. What created that valley, info about the salt lake, and how important the brine shrimp are. That sort of thing."

"Ah. I know just who you need." She pulled out her comm, tapping on the screen.

A series of chirps running up and down scales sounded behind them, and Sharon rolled her eyes. "Should have known. He's here."

An elderly K'Kat separated himself from the cluster of aides and runners against the wall, moving up behind them, an obviously amused expression on his face. "You rang?"

Sharon shook her head. "Darwin, can you three go somewhere Dad can get some questions answered? He has questions about the Green Bowl, among other things. If we need you, I'll call, so don't go too far, please? At least we have a chance of something happening soon. If this was a meeting on Earth, we'd be doing nothing but planning the agenda for the next one."

"Oh, I can assure you that such things never happen in the Empire, ma'am. After all, the Imperial government is fully capable of making a decision in minutes!" He grinned at the disbelief on their faces. "And if you believe that, I've got a brand new ship to sell you, cheap!"

Dan smiled widely, recognizing a kindred spirit. "Let's go find a place we can talk, Darwin." Turning, he said, "Sharon, call me if they get close to deciding anything. I have some thoughts."

"Sure thing. I'll just sit here getting bureaucrat's butt," Sharon replied with a snort. "Thanks, Dad."

"You'll get your exercise later, hon. I need to figure out if what I'm thinking of will work or not. I hope it does."

Sharon waved as the trio left the room, but Dan stopped them just outside the door. "Darwin, who would know about the vehicle the deputies are in? It looks like one of the Terran military scouts to me."

Ahleeah spoke up. "It is. A Terran Mark Twenty-Three, by the looks of it."

"How did you know... Never mind. Is it amphibious?"

"We rebuilt one in school. Class project. Yes, it can swim, but I'll have to check how fast it is in the water. It's propelled by the wheels, after all. You Terrans are strange."

"I think you've mentioned that before, darling."

"I have. And this thing you have with numbers..." She blushed. "Never mind."

"Okay. Check with the Sheriff's office, see how good of a condition their vehicle is in. If they know."

"What if they won't talk to me?"

"Claim Sharon sent you. She'll back you up on it."

"If you say so."

"I do." He took out his comm and typed rapidly, waiting mere seconds before a reply pinged. "Yep. She's sending you the same authority."

Ahleeah's comm pinged as well, and she looked at it in shock. "Full authority to inquire in this matter?"

"Yes, she trusts you. Family, y'know? You're her stepmother now, after all."

They allowed Darwin to lead them into a small room with a table and a few chairs, grabbing seats as Ahleeah pulled her closed headset from a pocket, turning away as she began paging through her comm in search of a code.

Dan looked across at the male K'Kat. "Sorry, I have to ask this. 'Darwin'? That sounds like a human name to me."

"It is. I took so many chances during the integration that the humans said I was going for a Darwin Award. I just never quite managed it. It became my nickname with the humans, and I decided to keep it."

Dan laughed with him, then sobered. "What can you tell me about the Green Bowl? How did it form? It looks almost like a maar eruption on the maps."

In the hallway, Stalker paused, listening, her ears swiveling. Yes, that was the voice of her new housemaker. The kind one. She could hear the voice of a furry one, as well. She knew that voice. The furry builder. The one her old housemaker had called "the crazy old man."

"Maar?"

"Volcanic ground water explosion. They leave holes like that."

"No, not volcanic. It's an old impact crater. We've never figured out how old it really is. Higher priorities, you know. But it predates the last ice age and is a lot deeper than it looks. It's filled in to maybe ninety percent of its original depth."

"And the exit canyon? Into the salt lake?"

"Erosion. Water running from the crater cut it when the ice sheets melted, we think."

"And the water in the crater?"

"It comes down through the strata from the mountains... Here, let me show you." Darwin powered up a screen on the wall, clicking rapidly through menus until a satellite view was shown, gesturing with a pointer that appeared on the screen. "Over here, as well as we can determine, is the source."

Dan looked at the scale in the corner of the view, then held up his fingers, measuring. "About sixty miles away, then."

"I guess? You humans and your measurements."

A scuttling noise drew her attention away from the voices and she froze in place, only the twitching of her ears betraying her interest as her head turned, smoothly, almost mechanically towards the interruption. There. One of the Old Prey, frozen by the magnificence of her gaze.

"And then twenty miles of open desert roadway to cross this pass to the Port. Is this as desolate as it looks, then?"

"Yes, and as dry. During the monsoon season, there is surface water, but it all runs into the lake."

"Then how did Morgana make it to the port? Cats aren't really made for traveling like that."

"She was riding in the cab of the truck, by the looks of things. The receiving crew remembers Franklin complaining at the dock about her riding in and deserting him."

Slowly, silently, she tested her footing, aligning her body with her target, a slow surge of tension filling her muscles before she exploded into motion, the despairing shriek of the Old Prey guiding her as surely as her own keen eyes through her two bounds, a strike of one clawed paw bouncing the mouse into the air, a second paw strike smashing it sideways to crash into a wall, stunned.

"And the salt levels in the lake itself?"

"They range from barely measurable at the inflow, low enough for the bulrushes to survive, to a saturated solution at the far side, where the salt precipitates out. The percentage rise is quite rapid."

"Interesting. Where does it reach three to five percent?"

Darwin zoomed the map in, indicating. "At this time of year, right about here."

Dan considered, estimating the distance. "About a quarter mile, then."

She hesitated, her paws pinning the Old Prey to the floor, its belly exposed to her teeth. Too easy.

"Ahleeah? How long would it take that vehicle to get to here?"

"About twenty to thirty minutes, I think. Maybe more. Captain Bowker's office staff says the scout car should be able to swim the lake."

First one, then the other paw lifted away from the Old Prey. Then, when it didn't move on its own, a swift strike sent it spinning.

"Hmm. See if you can reach Tahgaan. She should know how much power the point defense masers would need to reach the surface, and how widely the beams can be collimated."

"What exactly do you need to know?"

"How wide of a beam we can generate to hit the surface from orbit. And how much power we need to burn things there. I want to be able to boil water down to... Darwin, how deep are those ponds, do you know? Or can you find out?"

The Old Prey laid stunned for a moment, then drew its paws under itself, preparing to run.

Darwin shook his head. "Now I know why she grabbed me for this. Yes, I do know. The deepest ponds are right at two meters deep. Most of the rest are about one and a half. Franklin and I built them before he bought the place from me twenty years ago."

Stalker gathered herself as the Old Prey began to run, leaping into the air, her paws missing as it dodged the strike.

"One meter depth." He turned back to Darwin. "Then you know about the brine shrimp harvesting."

"Yes. We netted them to dry for fish food. Mostly for the Green Bowl; others, we trucked out. There are other fish farms, but none nearly as big."

"So we can lose that for a while."

"Yes."

She grabbed the Old Prey with a desperate sideways swipe of a clawed paw, feeling tiny bones crunch as she rolled with it, pinning it to the floor.

"Daan. Tahgaan says she can get an approximate fifteen-meter circle with 231's masers, and 111 can manage about the same. And put enough power on the surface to boil water as deep as you want to keep hitting it. Is that what you needed?"

"Perfect. How long would it take the ships to cover the bowl, the outflow, and the first four hundred yards offshore?"

Stalker looked at the tiny Old Prey, considering. It was broken. And she was hungry.

"She thinks, with all reactors up to run a full lateral line, along with the spinal and belly masers, two orbital passes for the two Nanokeets. She says that will give them a full double pass on each shoot."

"Even better. Thank you, and thank her for me."

Ahleeah giggled, then pulled her hushed mike away from her face. "She says you owe us a shopping trip to Karee's when we get back."

"Deal!"

The feline jaws descended and closed with rapid finality, Stalker's mouth welcoming the rush of hot, tasty blood. It washed away the disgusting taste of the New Prey. It was proper. Deserved. Welcomed. She held the body down with her paws as she crunched her way into her reward.

A few more minutes of discussion regarding water depths and outflows followed, until, "I think we have a plan. Let's go and present it, shall we?"

Darwin looked at him suspiciously. "Who is this 'we' you are talking about, human?"

"Me. You two just stand behind me and look pretty. Maybe spout a little technobabble to prove I'm not just a handsome guy with good hair, but totally crazy. You know, regular business pitch, high-level meeting style."

"I haven't ever done one of those."

Dan looked at him skeptically. "Sorry if I don't believe you." He turned his comm to show the information on the screen. "No one gets that much rank without doing a pitch meeting...Colonel."

Darwin froze. "I would appreciate your keeping that quiet, Mister Crane. In fact, I'd give much to know how you got that information? I'm not sure that even Pahrtul has it."

"He doesn't. And, well, I don't even tell myself half the things I know." He smiled. "At least, that's my story, and I'm sticking to it!"

Darwin shook his head again, then laughed and smiled. "I guess we shall present your plan, then." He extended a hand to Ahleeah, who looked up from her hushed headset in confusion. "Come with us, young one. You are about to learn the duties of an aide."

Dan led the way from their room, glancing at a chair, where a tail was swishing under it, smiling at the happy growling and crunching sounds.

"I guess Morgana found herself a snack, and I don't feel brave enough to interrupt her." He paused at the door to Operations. "Game faces on, folks. It's pitch time."

They walked into the room, listening with their backs against the wall to the discussion of the yield needed to sterilize the fish farm using an anti-shipping missile, before Dan cleared his throat.

Pahrtul looked at him quizzically, then nodded for him to speak.

"I have a proposal that doesn't involve nuclear devices, Captain Fahgian."

The virtual images of both captains turned towards him as he stepped into their views.

"Please explain this idea, Mister Crane. We would like to avoid nuking one of our own planets."

"Since I'm on that planet, so would I, sir. So would I."

Dan moved to the center of the table, a satellite image appearing on the screen behind him. In the projections of the conference, he could see both looking down at an echo of the screen. "What I propose, to sterilize the Green Bowl, is to use the point defense masers of the 231 and 111 to sweep the interior of the crater and down the exit to the main lake," he said.

Captain Fahgian looked up. "You do realize that the point defense has a beam the size of a human hand from orbit, correct? That will take hours, and penetrate very deeply into the ground beneath."

"True enough, sir, normally," Dan agreed. "However, Tahgaan informs me that there is also a training mode, for simulating ship-to-ship combat. It opens the beam to over one hundred times the normal diameter, and if the calculations are correct, should still be energetic enough to flash water into steam to a depth of well over a meter. Not to mention whatever else happens to be in it."

"If you got that information from Tahgaan, I will take her word for it," Fahgian replied thoughtfully. "How about the law enforcement people currently parked on our target? And the bodies of Mister Barnes and his people?"

"Sir, I'm afraid that we won't be able to recover Franklin Barnes or any other bodies. They will be cremated with the creatures that killed them."

"And the deputies?"

"That's even easier. It appears that a sufficient concentration of salt will kill Glass Lizards. They drive their vehicle straight into the salt lake, and head for the opposite shore. Once they are far enough away, the operation can begin. I would suggest that we hold our fire until they're at least halfway across the lake, since the second phase will begin with burning the shoreline within..." A line was drawn on the screen. "...About one hundred meters of the outlet, and proceed outwards from there. At least to the limits of the salt reeds..." Dan drew a second line on the screen, well outwards of the first, "...here."

Stalker finished cleaning her face with a paw and considered. Yes, her new housemaker could use her support. She silently approached the door, bumping her head against the leg of the furry one standing there to get his attention.

The guard at the door looked down, puzzled, taking in the sight of a cat standing on her hind legs, paws brushing at the door. He shrugged, opening the door for her. After all, the cats were killing the Glass Lizards. He wasn't going to obstruct one, at least not now.

Captain Fahgian frowned. "Will we have sufficient penetration to do what we need to do? And what about any vermin farther into the lake?"

Stalker halted, considering. Her housemaker was talking to...something. There were voices answering, but they came from the ceiling, like the sounds her old housemaker liked to listen to. Ah, well. She was Stalker of The New Prey; the voices would just have to manage.

"We've considered that. The maximum water depth within two hundred meters is rarely more than one meter, and never more than two. Also, any water we steam out in that area will be replaced by inflow from the rest of the lake, which is a much higher concentration of salt than we need to do the job."

"What about this vegetation in the initial band, then?"

"It might survive, it might not. It's Tychae family, Terran ca... Bulrushes. No one is even sure how it got there."

"I see. Let me verify the information on salt killing Lizards and draw up a fire plan. We'll get back to you, Mister Crane."

She leapt onto the table, flowing over it onto the arm of her housemaker, up, and onto his shoulder, her proper place. She pressed her cheek against his ear, and purred.

Captain Fahgian leaned in toward his pickup. "Is that cat yours?"

"Yes, apparently. She has decided she is, at any rate."

"Are you planning to bring her aboard with you, then?"

"If she'll come, sir. She...ah...seems to have adopted me. Pending approval, of course!"

"Is this the one who killed the first of our little problems?"

"She is."

"Then I will give tentative approval, if Doctor Rogattin checks her out first."

"Of course, sir, though we're under quarantine down here, so..."

"Of course. Let's get that lifted. Stay close. Director Pahrtul will have to give the final approval for the operation, of course."

Dan nodded, gathering up his two companions with a look. "We'll be across the hall if you have questions."

"It seems straightforward enough. By the way, Mister Crane?"

"Yes, Captain?"

"You seem to have a talent for collecting female cats."

Ahleeah giggled as Dan winced. "Aye, Captain."

Twenty minutes went by, with Morgana receiving her due number of pets and scritches, before dropping bonelessly into Dan's lap.

At last, there came a knock at the door, followed by a head. "Director's compliments, Mr. Crane. Can you come back to Ops, please?"

With a wince, they rose, following Dan back.

"Yes, Director?"

"Approved. Since it's your plan, you get to explain their part to our deputies on the scene."

"Ah. Hopefully they don't shoot the messenger?"

"Something like that. Besides, you'll be offplanet shortly. And I can blame you for anything that goes wrong."

"Ah! Delegation!"

"Exactly! Much easier for me if you aren't here to explain yourself."

"Let's get them on screen, then. If my orbital mechanics are right, the ships will be overhead in an hour or so."

"Actually, slightly more than that. The 231 is staying in an Equatorial orbit and 111 is shifting to a Polar. It has to do with with the geometry of the sides of the bowl." He frowned. "I was Logistics, not combat. It makes sense to me, but I can't really explain it very well."

"Sir, I'll leave that to the captains. After all, shooting things was their job!"

⁂

Jim stared at Dan in disbelief. "You want us to do...what, again?"

"Drive your patrol vehicle straight out across the lake. It's amphibious, right?"

"It *was* amphibious. We haven't tested that in years."

"Hmm. Well, what's the worst than can happen, then?"

"It sinks and we drown?"

"Jim, I've got a question for you."

"What's that? I mean, I would really like to survive this, Mister Crane."

"You grew up in North America, yes?"

"Yeah, why?"

"Did you ever go to the Great Salt Lake up in Utah?"

"Yes, I did."

"Did you go swimming?"

"No, we just drove across it."

"That lake has so much salt in it that a human actually has to swim downwards to go underwater."

"I see."

"Did you ever swim in the ocean? Notice how much easier it was to float?"

"Kinda."

"Same thing here, only more so."

"If you say so."

"Trust me, Jim."

"You're from the government and you're here to help, right?

Dan laughed. "And the check is in the mail!"

"And you promise you won't..." A quick sideways glance stopped the deputy midsentence. "Nevermind... Okay. Looks like the only way out. We've been sitting here for hours now. We'll go for it."

"You've got about forty-three minutes by my clock before the ships can hit the crater."

"Yup." The sounds of a motor starting came over the link, and the view rocked randomly from side to side. "What do we do when we get to the other side?"

"Get back in the water to soak your uniforms and gear, to kill any eggs or larvae."

"I...see. And if we sink on the way?"

"Trigger an upload on your electronics, strip down and swim for it."

On the monitor, Jim shook his head sadly. "Even if we will float, that is not an encouraging Plan B."

"Better than trying to swim in your uniforms, Deputy!"

"I know. Doesn't mean I have to like it."

The view stabilized, splashes of mud visible on the side windows of the scout car.

"We're...moving kinda slow here, Boss. Are we going to have time?"

Dan looked up from his own comm. "Hopefully. Captain Tomeck wants to use his equipment to breach the dams in the fish farm. Calibration shots. He's concerned about being able to target through smoke and steam."

"How were they going to do that, anyways? Radar?"

"No, the Captains say they want to offset from Spaceport Control's transmitter, and the beacon at the stockyards."

"That seems...a little crazy there, boss."

"*Nanokeet*-class ships, Deputy. Nothing normal about them at all. Ask me how I know."

An engine roared in the background. Open water. "You work on one, Mister Crane. I guess you would!"

"But they're such glorious ships, Deputy!"

"Oh, no question of that. I wish this scout car was, though. It's leaking. And the pumps aren't handling all of it." The engine labored for a moment, then steadied. "Looks like we found some bottom. Have to see how long that lasts."

A distinctly feminine voice chimed in. "These are my favorite boots, too! Well, were, I guess."

"Sorry. One-Eleven is overhead. You might want to trigger uploads while you have the chance, including your comms. They'll sequester the data for you."

Stalker of the New Prey raised her head, hearing the distress in the new voice. Her housemaker remained calm, still stroking her back. She rolled under his hand, feeling him scritch her belly. She briefly considered grabbing the hand. No. This felt good. Maybe another time.

In orbit, the pair of four hundred meter-long ex-military support ships rolled their side batteries into alignment with the surface of the planet, upper, lower, and broadside masers swiveling in unison, seeking their targets.

That female voice again. "Promise?"

"Yes. It will go into the same system that handles secure message traffic. I promise. Just set it for an encrypted, long-transmission-delay data-dump."

Seconds later, the ping of Transfer Complete sounded.

"That was fast!"

"Big receiving dishes, Deputy!"

"Hmm."

"Yes, best not to speculate."

Several bright flashes washed out the visual transmission from the scout car, followed by a chorus of, "What was *that*?"

"One-Eleven calibrating her guns." A long pause. "Looks like she was off by fifty millimeters, according to her message traffic." A longer pause. "Guns is concerned."

Dan could see Jim's hand covering his face for a moment. "Error of fifty millimeters. From how high? And he's concerned about that?"

"She. And yes, she is. K'Kats get that way, you know. Even running firing solutions from three hundred fifty klicks up. It makes them look bad."

The engine sounds raced for a moment, they gradually wound back down. "Lost our bottom there. Swimming again."

"It's fine, you have at least another orbit, a bit under ninety minutes. The Lizards aren't going anywhere, and Tomeck wants to adjust."

The engine noise rose, fell, sputtered, stopped. "Well, at least we have bottom under us again."

"Problem?"

"Looks like water in the electronics bay, from the way all of the readouts are flashing. Radios are at the top of the compartment with the batteries under them. Looks like we might have to wade for it."

"From your last position, about a mile to the shore?"

"Yes."

"Want some advice?"

"I suspect I know what it is, but sure."

"Strip down, grab your survival packs, leave your boots behind, put on extra socks, and start going. Any extra drinking water you have in the vehicle, drink it now. Don't wait around."

"Why the hurry?"

"Because that lake is going to get very rough in a bit, and clothes and boots will slow you down way too much."

The female voice Dan now knew as Blake spoke up. "I am *not* happy about this! I did *not* sign up to run around mostly naked in the sun! Among other things, I tend to sunburn easily."

"Do you have a reflector blanket in your pack?"

"Of course! I'm not an idiot!"

"Get it out first, then reseal your pack. Once you are away from the car, drape it like a poncho. It'll save your skin. Besides, once the ships start firing, it'll get cloudy. Now get going!"

In the transmission from the car, the view shifted to outside, and muttered words came over the audio, followed by splashes, curses, and thumps. Two figures came into view hip-deep in the water, one balding, one with hair so blonde it was nearly white, wrapped in reflective blankets.

Each turned, obviously looking back past the scout car, then forward, repeating until the woman turned to the man. "Third peak from the left?"

"And straight on until morning! Boss? Do you have our beacons?"

Dan looked to his left, getting a nod from the sensor tech. "Looks like both of them."

"We're off. We'll leave the link switched on here. Wish us luck!"

"Good luck."

Dan leaned back in his chair, glancing at Darwin and Ahleeah, who had been quietly chatting during the exchange. He shook his head slowly, "I hate waiting."

Darwin nodded. "I know that feeling. You want to be out there with them."

He nodded back, watching the slow crawl of the beacon markers after the wading figures had disappeared into the haze. Finally. "Yes."

Stalker of the New Prey could feel the tension through her housemaker's touch, and stood, lightly patting his cheek to get his full attention. When he looked down at her, she nuzzled his cheek. She trusted this one. He would provide a safe house for her and her soon-to-be kittens.

Speaking of kittens... She flowed off her housemaker's lap, padding to the door. Either of those bold Hunters would make marvelous babies with her. It was time to find one of them. After all, a Stalker had her priorities!

Pahrtul sat down heavily, sighing. "Looks like our pests did come in with a delivery of fish. In the ice, to be exact."

Darwin glanced at Dan, receiving a nod in return. "We have confirmed this?"

"Bio has a scanner that can follow the chemical trail of them. They have confirmed that there are no more in the Complex, and all traces they can find have ended in dead Glass Lizards in trashcans, toilets, or flowerbeds. Those Terran cats are certainly...efficient at eliminating enemies. Now I know why you humans like them!"

Dan laughed. "Well, not all humans. Just the smart ones!" More soberly, "Do we know where the infestation came from?"

Pahrtul nodded. "We've narrowed it down to a water freezing unit delivered here several months ago. The Kor-Can representative is contacting Imperial Naval Intelligence to trace where it came from, but I suspect some sort of fiction in the documentation of it."

"If Medical can give us clean scanner records, maybe we can get the quarantine lifted. I was worried about that, to be honest. I would hate to have our ship leave without us!"

"As would I, Mister Crane. As would I."

Dan gave him a sly grin. "Ah, admit it! You just don't want to tell the deputies who *really* authorized the plan to send them for a swim!"

⁂

In the end, the operation was simultaneously spectacular and anticlimactic. The horizon behind the scout car erupted in multicolored lightning, followed many seconds later by a continuous rumble of thunder, lasting for several minutes as the sources of the lightning moved across the sky.

Minutes later, a wave slowly washed against the back of the scout car, then dragged it backwards as a tremendous cloud boiled into the sky.

The Operations crew listened to the comm chatter between the ships, their shuttle crews, and ground control, before the orbits of the ships brought them over the bowl and lake again, and a second storm of strobing lights and thunder began.

⁂

Three days later, standing on the receiving area of the spaceport runway, Dan leaned over and pressed his lips between Ahleeah's ears. "Soon, darling. We will go back to our home."

As the shuttle rolled to a stop, she raised her face, kissing his lips in return. "Yes, love. Soon."

From Dan's shoulder, Morgana purred.

Milky Way Moggie

RITA BEEMAN

YOU MIGHT NOT KNOW it to look at me, but I carry the load that has burdened trailblazers since time immemorial. It's true that I wear it well. Oh, my languorous beauty gives the air of unconcern and voluptuousness, but I take seriously my sacred place and duties in the order of things. I also take seriously my pleasures. When possible, I combine duty with pleasure. I keep a meticulous toilet. You dirty humans really should try licking your paws and cleaning your heads. Then again, you're not very attractive with all that bald hide of yours, so you just go around dirty. Sorry you lost the fur lottery, suckers.

I was born here, out at the edge of all things, in a dark little cubby on this vast starship. Mother gave me and my littermates precious milk that made me grow strong and flexible. I am as much a warrior as a lover of life. I require my strength and flexibility for all these pursuits. One day soon, I will whelp a litter of my own. I'd watched for a suitable candidate to sire my first litter. I was mostly underwhelmed by the candidates in this zone of the ship. Until recently, I'd just enjoyed the prowl.

Oh, and cunning. Did I mention my cleverness? Well, it must be apparent, but in case you lack the intelligence to discern how clever I am, I must declare myself. My beauty is only excelled by my wit. Do not trifle with me.

My mother gave me a name, but you would not be able to say it. You may call me Boudicca. Enough of your human lore has survived that I understand the meaning of this name, and the provenance befits me. Your kind love this convergence of characteristics in my kind. You love our beauty and cunning, and you love when we exasperate you. Silly humans. Still, you amuse, so I suppose we will continue to indulge you. How lucky you are.

You perhaps may not know the history, how my kind was welcomed on seafaring vessels on the origin planet. I see you shaking your head, but it's absolutely true! Vermin thrived on the comestibles locked deep in the dark holds of ancient ships. Rats. Mice. Even small bugs mesmerize my kind, and we are driven to kill in all cases. We may or may not eat the objects of our obsession, but we do so love to play with our food. One must enjoy the simple pleasures in life. I digress. Throughout humanity's history of boating for conquest, boating for pleasure, boating for sport, they have wisely recognized the importance of their alliance with my kind on their vessels, and in exchange, we live well and mostly stay off the menu.

Humans are a warmongering lot, and they learned the best of their practices from my kind. Stealth is what they learned from observing us. Stalking is an art which we perfected even before your kind evolved to your current form. Smoothness is crucial. Our every move is essential. We glide slowly, slowly, ever so quietly, until we move like a flash and then *pounce*!

One must admit that rodents are tremendous survivors and can slip through impossibly small spaces. In this way, we have not managed to eradicate their species. Still, it would be a shame to wipe them out entirely, as they do amuse. Perhaps that's why rats do not evolve—why should they? Likewise for my kind. If you had a perfectly preserved rat specimen from ancient earth ships and compared it to a rat of this age, they would be indistinguishable. Brown rat. Street rat. Wharf rat. Space station rat. What did I tell you? Survivors. They are clever enough.

Oh, about the ship: I mentioned its vastness. Only in a ship of this size could diversity of our bloodlines be managed through the centuries. Still, ones such as Mother produce many broods. However, most of them do not survive adolescence. Recently, the ship has ventured to a neighboring star system in the Milky Way to drop off a load of cargo. Sometimes we pick up more than we offload. One recent port of call infected the ship with tiny terrors that prey upon ones such as my fair self. The slow and simple will not survive, but it was ever thus. I mean to survive.

There we were, docked to the port on a vast space station just yesterday. Inevitably, rats come and rats go on the underside of the gangplank. Think of them as a free-ranging version of your human herpes. You humans have spent countless credits on devices to keep the dock rats out and the ship rats in, but they find workarounds. Their sharp teeth are models of efficiency when it comes to defeating gaskets, rubber cowlings, and other mechanisms meant to block their passage. The gangplank itself has a hygiene mechanism that zaps and fries any rodent that crosses it, so they quickly adapted to engineer workarounds on the underside. Every fix the humans come up with will stick for a brief while, but is soon defeated. The humans counteract this by making their stops at ports as brief as possible. Well, they try, anyway.

The problem yesterday came from one of those very breaches. The rats bored a hole from both sides of the cowling, and no sooner had the hole appeared than a giant unicellular ciliate came oozing through the gap, followed by unctuous blobs of a dozen or so of its closest and best friends. Mind you, these blobs were about the size of a moggie, but they squeezed their boneless forms through impossibly small holes.

There's a lot to be said for tucking in and tackling a challenge head-on, but sometimes it's best to assess before you make a hasty choice. Remember that bit about stealth? If you're going to take a stand, best to not let them see you setting up to wallop them.

A scruffy pack of bachelor cats rolled up and poofed up proper, ready to kick some blob booty. The blobs didn't care. A pal of mine, Pauline, watched from behind a crate as a phalanx of cats faced off with the advancing squish of blobs. They said the blobs had no obvious vocal mechanism, but she swears that one of them said, "Here, kitty-kitty!"

That shit really pisses us off, by the way.

Anyway, the gang of cats dove right in, and the fur was flying. Talons and teeth flashed, blobs and cats all turned into a roiling, churning mess of slime and hissing, but soon devolved into a pitiful sight. Pauline said the cat gang never had a chance. The moggies fought valiantly, but as soon as a blob found purchase on fur, they began to enfold the cat, quickly encasing them, and digesting them with remarkable speed, after which each blob divided into two. We all—moggie and human alike, I suspect—owe our survival to Pauline. She said once touched by the edge of the blobs, a cat could not extract itself, and died a quick but messy and excruciating death. The yowling of the dying cats had echoed throughout that sector of the ship, and then the humans were involved. The first human to arrive on the scene was horrified and took a pushbroom to the shapeless mass. He managed to bust a couple blobs open, but he was quickly overwhelmed by blobs glomming onto his workboots and traveling up his legs. They sort of ate him from the ground up. Several blobs glommed onto the brushes of the broom, and traveled up the handle with remarkable speed, and onto the arm of the man. He took a little longer to digest than the cats, but Pauline said his shrieks sounded almost respectably catlike.

Pauline leapt up to an air vent and raced to the food hold where most of the cats lurked to tell them what had happened on the dock. Being the supreme beings on board, the feline consortium quickly surmised that these menacing blobs were impervious even to the loud, odious weapons of the humans on board. The blobs would slime their way around the ship, devouring and dissolving both man, rat, and cat, and what were we to do?

I was in the engine room—rats like the warmth there—when I heard a kerfuffle. A terrorized pack of kittens came tearing through the room, and I scooped one up by the scruff and growled at her through my teeth to tell me what was going on. What came out of her mouth was hysterical nonsense, and I shook her gently, not enough to snap her spine, but enough to let her know I was in control. She calmed enough to tell me that some scary blobby things were eating people and cats, and please don't make her go back there. I knew something seriously jacked was afoot, but I would not be the fool who rushed in.

I took a beat to collect my thoughts and review all Mother's training. Mother's rules for engagement were: keep yourself tidy so you are at your most beautiful while you are kicking ass; let the morons run in first; watch what happens to the morons; let the morons resolve it, if possible, because it's probably naptime; and shut that shit down, if you must.

I checked myself. Yes, still beautiful and clean. Maybe a few more contemplative swipes at my whiskers. There, that's better. Apparently, the morons had already rushed in. Yes, apparently the morons had paid the ultimate price, alas. It was definitely my naptime, but the problem resolved the morons, not vice-versa. I'd better tuck in and see what I could do about this, because I had precisely zero intention of getting smoked by a bunch of slimeballs while I was in an as-yet-un-deflowered state. No way was I going to let my virginity go down with the ship.

I took a beat to wonder if Mother might be on the scene, but then remembered that the recreational deck still had an infestation of those tenacious little weevils that hopped on at a port in the Proxima Centauri system. She had a new batch of kittens in the oven and had a particular taste for those weevils. Said she likes the crunch. I guess Mother wouldn't be helping out with this battle, and hopefully the blobs would never make it to that deck, one of the uppermost of the ship.

I stalked out into the central passage as rats, more juveniles of my species, and a few random odd creatures came running up the corridor. I noted the chaos, considered it, and let it rush past, vowing not to be swept along the frantic wave.

I walked calmly, assessing the state of the terrorized creatures that rushed towards me, when I noticed a presence, a large black cat keeping pace with me on the opposite side of the corridor. I knew his name. You couldn't pronounce it. I'll call him Julius. I'd seen him about, but we'd never spoken. He was sleek, black, young and muscular. Terror was on the line, but I confess for a moment I thought about asking if he found me beautiful. I didn't need to ask, though. His smoldering amber eyes flashed at me, and I nodded. We walked calmly, smoothly. I'd been in a few scraps before, but this would be my first real test. Julius, on the other hand, seemed like he'd done this before. We padded silently along the corridor, sidestepping the occasional bottle brush-tailed, wild-eyed kittens that came hurtling up the passage.

"This way," said Julius, as he pointed his chin up to a ventilation tube six feet off the ground. I knew it well, knew we could follow it to the artery of vents over the cargo area.

He was a cooler cat than I knew was possible. In fact, the look in his eye made me think he'd been thinking about my romantic future.

"I've noticed you. Boudicca, right?"

"How did you know?"

"I asked around. I am partial to a calico girl, and your green eyes...well, I noticed them."

"Don't get ahead of yourself, boy," I said. I heard his low chuckle that was just on the cusp of a purr, but I was secretly pleased that he'd been interested enough to ask around about me. I wouldn't tell him that I knew his name, but I didn't have to ask around for it. Word gets around, is all. I wouldn't dream of snooping overtly for information on a male cat. Tabbies are everywhere, and they are the biggest gossips imaginable, especially the gingers. Plus, a girl has her ego to consider. Virago warrior calicos like me are uncommon. Best he consider me on a pedestal, even if we are about to die.

"A kitten told me some blobby things are eating cats and humans at the main cargo deck. She said one eats a cat, then divides into two blobs. This sounds like a tricky situation."

"It does."

"Fortunately, we're tricky. Right?"

Came that low purr chuckle again, and I fancy he winked at me. "Right," he said. Oh no. Turns out I'm seriously a sucker for those golden amber eyes. Something in me wants to stop right here and dispense with the virginity, but then again, it would be a shame to have all that fun and then be snuffed out right away. Besides, I don't want it to seem too easy for him. He probably has a lot of tail thrown his way, and I'm not just any hussy-cat. The last thing I want is a mess of stupid blob-fodder kittens.

The oncoming traffic in the ventilation shaft was considerably less than that of the corridor, but the ones coming through were clearly aghast. Some keened a chattering nonsense that was more unsettling than any collection of words might have been. I remembered my training, determined to make Mother proud.

We turned the corner to the tube that led to the catwalks above the cargo area, and the sight below was astonishing. Arrayed along the catwalks were dozens of our kind, the fighting class of feline, both male and female, every color and every stripe of cat. They watched below as more humans from the ship hastened into the arena with the blobs. Even when a human or cat managed to breach the membrane of one of those things, they were quickly attacked by more blobs, who turned into even more blobs. The attrition rate for the ship's denizens was outpaced by the accretions of the growing sea of blobs.

All the while, there was a chatter among the moggies on the catwalk, discussing what might be done. Up here, we were safe from the reach of the blobs, but we couldn't stay here forever. Furthermore, we're cats, which means we are expert at deploying and interpreting stink, but the stench of the ghastly fumes from dissolving lifeforms was hideous, and did the opposite of bolstering our spirits.

Now let me take a moment to surprise you by admitting that cats understand the intricacies of physics, all forms of mathematics (we are born calculating angles—hello, we land on our feet, *always*), and chemistry. We just don't care. We therefore understood well that something of the caustic nature of the guts of these blobs could well be the undoing of the very vessel that stood between us and the quick but cruel death one might enjoy in space. This was serious business. Despite not caring about physics, math, and chemistry, we have enough sense to deploy any or all of these to save our own magnificent behinds. The oldest and wisest of our number stood at a corner on the treadplate, looking down occasionally, and discussing what was to be done.

Julius, however, was impatient. He kept looking at me, but it was to his credit that he did not attempt to mollycoddle me by seeing if I was all right. The last thing I wanted was to be treated as fragile and frightened. I was mad as, well, a wet cat. They had utterly ruined my naptime. I sensed him glance in my direction one more time, and I turned my head and locked eyes with Julius. I was seriously pissed. As if rehearsed, we both narrowed our eyes, angry. I felt my lip curl slightly to reveal one of my lovely, long pointy teeth.

Julius seemed to read my mind, when suddenly, he said, "Screw this!" He walked deliberately to the catwalk that spanned the center of the cargo space, lifted his leg, and let fly a magnificent arc of urine from his impressively overstuffed bladder, spattering his disdain over the mass of blobs below.

To the amazement of all, not the least of which was the blobs, their membranes burst at first contact with the golden shower from Julius. A growl of awe susurrated all along the catwalk, from which myriad arcs of yellow erupted onto the panicking mass of blobs below. I confess I even let fly a dainty stream of my own piss. It was beautiful. Julius let forth a yowl of victory as the ciliate bags burst on the floor all around, their caustic guts neutralized (or overpowered) by the magical properties of cat pee. I knew then that Julius would give me smart babies with a better-than-average chance of survival.

So, yeah. I could have cowered in the grub hold awaiting death or deliverance, but that's not the kind of moggie I am. If I'm going to go, I'm going to go out swinging, clawing, biting and hissing. And that's what I want in the sire of my dreams. A muscular black cat that doesn't shrink from a fight is just the sire for me. Our babies will teach their babies, and they'll sail on other ships to systems we can't begin to imagine, because, truly, the logistics don't matter when there's naps to be had and babies to be made. We don't care about that stuff. We are warriors, and piss on anything that tries to stop us.

Mother will be so proud.

Moggie Clawbearer

SARAH ARNETTE

It was a busy life I led, prowling the ship and checking on my charges. They were a hard bunch to watch over. There was never enough time to get to all of them, but they all needed my personal attention. After all, it was the mental health of those around me that I was supposed to be guarding with my life, and that was not a vocation to be taken lightly. I was a Feline Companion Morale Specialist. I attended to every Marine on this ship, even if they were not all my clients. There were other Feline Companion Moral Specialists on this ship, but I was the Head of the Department.

I must've been getting tired, because one of my charges managed to sneak up behind me and scooped me up into a hug: Private John Lees. Seriously, someone should put a bell on him. He was new to the ship, so he didn't understand that scooping up an officer for a cuddle was rather inappropriate. He didn't do this to the other officers on the ship, though—just me. It might've been a species thing, but he would have to understand that I was an officer, even though I was also a cat. Cuddles were one thing, but consent was absolutely necessary, and maybe a little warning would've been nice.

That's right: I, Major Moggie Clawbearer, am a cat. I still have a beautiful tortoise-shell coloration, but you can only see it on my head and paws. The rest of me was covered up with my space uniform, a light gray one-piece with the appropriate cut-outs. The only other thing I wore was my translation collar, which translated my words to those that humans could understand. My rank and insignia were stitched to my back and chest, making it easy for people to see who they were dealing with. Not that most people need to be reminded that I am an officer...just John Lees.

I didn't struggle in Private Lees's embrace. He needed a lot of attention, and he received a lot of joy in cuddling me and the other cats on the ship. He had often stated that he had a lot of cats at his home, back before he joined the Space Marines, Earth Division. It could be hard for the Earthborn to understand that their cats were different from Space Cats like myself. We looked a lot alike, but there were several major differences.

The primary difference between the space cat and the Earth Cat was that the Space Cat was smarter. We were genetically bred to be smarter than your average cat. We had to be smarter, since we were expected to handle the rigors of space and all that entailed. We had also been genetically engineered to live longer and be healthier than your average cat. We were a little bit bigger, too, ranging between twenty to thirty Earth pounds. All of this was to make us better adapted to space and our primary mission; to keep the worlds safe for everyone.

Once Private Lees put me back down, I walked off, keeping my tail high and head erect. I couldn't let him know that part of me favored him over the rest of the crew, if only because he was so free with his affections. With a glance at the clock, I started to jog off in the direction of the Bridge. We were due to arrive at the Space Station Starpath for resupply and revelry. I, for one, was excited to get off the ship for a minute.

I barely made it in time before they locked the doors. They did this every time we engaged with another body in space, and the reason was pretty simple: whenever we locked onto another body, there were a few moments of weightlessness while we synced up to their gravity. If there was going to be a problem with pressure or fire, it would happen in those moments.

Locking the doors shut helped to prevent those problems from spreading to the rest of the ship. Granted, these problems hadn't occurred in the past fifty years, but there was no reason to stop being careful.

I slipped in just as the doors began to shut, being careful not to let my tail get caught. I could only imagine how humiliating it would've been to delay our approach because the doors had to be opened to let my tail through. Captain Kostova would've never let me live that down. With a single bound, I took my place next to the Captain's Chair and listened as the announcements regarding our approach were made.

"All hands, all hands, prepare for gravity to disengage. Weightlessness to occur in one minute," was the first announcement. The crew should've already been buckled down and had everything stowed in a safe place. We had been planning to approach Starpath at this exact time for over twenty-four hours, and we gave a lot of warning in advance. No one should be caught off guard, not to say that the one-minute warning wasn't helpful for those who lost track of time. At the second announcement, giving the crew the thirty-second marker, Captain Kostova clipped me to my spot, anchoring me in place.

"Zero Gravity in five...four...three...two...one...and zero gravity achieved," the ship announced. At the Zero Gravity Achieved marker, I felt all the weight of gravity lift from me, and I rose slightly out of my seat. The buckle that the captain attached to me helped to hold me in place and kept me safe in case there were any sudden movements by the ship. Looking around, I can see that everyone else was safely buckled into their seats, as well. I could only assume that the rest of the ship was equally well-secured. If not, the Captain and the Chief of Security, Lackey, would take care of them.

Zero gravity was actually why cats were in space and not dogs. Yeah, on land and in places where gravity was constant, dogs might be man's best friend, but in space, it was cats. We were far more superior to dogs when it came to dealing with changes in gravity. Our ability to always land on our feet helped us navigate a zero-gravity situation and fall safely if we were caught unawares when gravity came back on. They tried dogs, but dogs simply weren't able to catch themselves like cats could.

"Connection to Space Station Starpath successful. Matching gravity in five...four...three...two...and one. Gravity at One G," the Communications Officer announced as gravity was restored. Captain Kostova unclipped me from my seat as he had the crew verify that there were no complications before releasing those of us with shore leave to our own recognizance.

⁂

Private Lees was in his dress uniform when he met me at the bay doors. While most officers were not encouraged to fraternize with non-officers, my position didn't have the same restrictions. Feline Companion Morale Specialists were expected to be friends with everyone. Today, he and I were heading out for some sushi and shopping. I greatly missed fresh sushi. The reconstituted stuff that we had on the ship was simply not the same, even though they claimed it was.

Perched on Private Lees's shoulders, we quickly made it through the commercial district of the Starpath. From my vantage point, I could see the entire floor, which was shaped like a giant square. Each wall led to landing bays for the various ships. The area right by the landing bays was wide open for security precautions. There were elevators at the corners of these walls that allowed the Starpath civilians on and off the floor, but they were off-limits to us and to other space travelers. It kept the station safer that way. The only downside to this location was how bright it was. The walls were white, and so was the ceiling. Pair that with bright LED lights, and the room was almost blindingly bright.

The center area of the room was the important part. That was where all the restaurants, stores, and booths were set up. These were specifically set up for space travelers, and while station citizens could eat and shop here, most of them avoided this area altogether. The only ones who routinely came to this floor were the ones who worked here. The size of this space was deceptive. It might look like it was a hundred square yards in size, but I knew for a fact that it was over two miles across to the other side of the room. It was just a perspective issue.

The sushi bar that we were planning on going to was in the middle of the room, about a mile away. It was a well-appointed place called the Cosmic Fish. It boasted the largest selection of fresh fish in the quadrant, and they backed that claim up by having live fish vats where you could actually watch the fish swim as you ate. I had made sure that we had reservations for the place months ago.

Sitting down at a booth that their waiter showed us to, Lees and I got a chance to look around the place. The lights were comfortably dimmed, providing a stark contrast to the bright and almost glaring lights from the ceiling outside of the restaurant. They managed this feat by placing awnings above the booths, giving the place an outside feel, even though you were soundly inside a building, really a building in another building. The sensation was further enhanced by the controlled application of a breeze with the artificial scent of an Earthside ocean. The only thing lacking was the artificial bird calls. The booths might've been made of a plast-steel, but they were dressed up to look like real wood. It was little wonder that this place was one of the most expensive sushi restaurants on the station.

After enjoying a platter with a sampling of sushi, red bean buns, and real rice, Lees and I had to admit that we were full and ready to head back to the ship. We had twenty-two more standard hours of revelry, but it had been a long day and we'd had a filling meal. It was time for some rest, and then we would explore the shops tomorrow. There was plenty of time.

Lees and I decided to avoid the busy streets that were the direct route from the Cosmic Fish and the ship. Instead, we headed towards the bulk foods section first, off to the left-hand corner of the marketplace. It was a longer but far less busy route, making it faster, or so we assumed.

For Coda Paws, this day could not possibly get much worse. It started out with the ship being late for its landing pass. They'd had some engine trouble en route, and that put them behind schedule by a day. This meant that they took a penalty on their shipments. Now their supplier was trying to sabotage their grain shipment by forcing them to take grain that had been contaminated by mice.

"Captain, we cannot take these oats. They won't pass inspection," Paws tried to impress upon Jack Brown, the owner and captain of the ship Paws was working on, the *Peacetime*. They were a small-time shipping business, and Paws had been with Brown for a very long time—his entire life, if he had to be honest about it.

"You're overreacting, the grain is fine," the merchant was telling Brown, overriding Paws's objections.

"I can smell the mice," Paws all but growled. He was sitting on Brown's shoulder, making him eye-level with the merchant, whose name he did not get. He preferred to be on Brown's shoulders, especially when the merchant also happened to have a dog, a big dog. Paws had managed to get the dog's name, Brava, and just as the name sounded, he was a big, mean-looking dog.

"You smell my daughter's mice. She is always bringing them to my shop. That does not mean that the grain is infested or that it will not pass inspection. Besides, you don't have a choice. You must accept my grain. No one else has anything to ship out, and you were late. Either take the grain or leave the station empty. It's up to you," the merchant said, turning his gaze first to Paws, and then to Brown. The threat was evident: either they bought from him, or he would make it impossible for them to buy from anyone else.

"We'll leave it. I trust Coda. He says this is bad grain, then it's bad grain. Goodbye, Stone," Brown said, keeping a steady eye on the merchant, ignoring Brava altogether. With that, Brown turned around and walked away from the stall and the gaylord of grain that he was expecting to load onto his ship.

"Thank you for trusting me," Coda said as he held onto Brown's shoulder.

"You're my crew, my cat. You might be young, but that does not make you incompetent. I'm going to trust you until you show me that I cannot trust you," Brown answered as they walked. They had to find another vendor, fast. Stone, the merchant, was not bluffing when he said that they might have to leave empty, but Brown had a plan. He might have to pay more for the grain, but he knew another merchant who would sell to him. Their profits would not be as high, but it would be better than flying empty or taking a penalty for trying to ship in contaminated grain. Within twenty minutes, they had a new deal and safe grain being delivered to the ship immediately.

❧ ⸙ ☙

Lees and I were just passing the area when we heard the Lawdogs barking. These were the Starpath's security dogs. They were smarter than Earth dogs, fully capable of communication and investigations. They typically worked with a human, but there had been past instances where they worked alone or in pairs sans the human. While the smart move would have been to keep walking away from the disturbance and towards our ship, we instead decided to investigate.

The scene before us was just finishing up. We saw a Starpath officer handcuffing a man, a merchant marine, by the looks of it, and a shipment of grain being impounded. The man was not fighting the officer, but instead insisting that there had been some sort of mistake. He paid for safe grain, not the rot that they had tried to load onto his ship. Just as we were about to leave, a young cat stepped into our path.

"Please, you've got to help me. They're taking my captain away," the cat pleaded with us. He was a young cat, barely a teenager in human equivalent years. His big eyes took up almost half of his face, making him look even younger. His tiger-striped fur was clearly evident, with the cat wearing nothing more than a translation collar and a jean jacket. He looked desperate because he *was* desperate.

"Why don't you tell me what is going on," I suggested as I jumped off Lees's shoulder. This young cat might not be my crew, but I still felt the need to provide comfort and assistance. I knew Lees would feel the same way. We sat down in front of the cat and waited expectantly.

Coda began to explain what had happened with Stone and the threat that he made. Then he explained how they then bought fresh grain from another vendor, Crown, but that this was not the grain that they had bought. This was the first grain, from Stone. He did not know where the grain from Crown was, and since the paperwork looked legitimate, the Lawdogs arrested Brown for attempting to buy contaminated grain to be sold as fresh grain at an outpost.

"Well, it sounds like the answer is simple," Lees said, as Coda finished explaining. "We're going to have to find the grain you bought from Crown and figure out how they switched the grain. That way you guys can ship out with the right product and on time. It's expensive to ship out late." I had to agree with him that we at least had to attempt to find the good grain and help our new friend.

"I'm betting that Stone has it," Coda said, when Lees asked him for his opinion as to where the grain went.

"Well, that is the first place we'll have to look," Lees suggested. "But first, we need a disguise. There is no one who would believe that a couple of military ship personnel are going to be on the hunt for grain to sell.

"Right, disguises..." Lees said as he began to rub his chin in thought. I knew this was going to be a bad idea, even before it fully formed in Lees's brain.

It was a horribly bad idea, but it might work. I half-stripped out of my uniform, rolling the top of it down to just below my ribs, hiding all of the insignias and markings that gave me away as an officer. Lees simply raided his new friend's captain's wardrobe, selecting loose-fitting clothing and a backpack to carry his uniform. Scruffing up our hair a bit and double-checking for any type of identification, we headed off to Stone's, with Coda in the lead.

When we made it to Stone's shop, we found it locked. It was pretty late in station time, so it made sense that the place was locked up for the shift, especially since they were not expecting anyone. The lock did not stop Lees. "Close your eyes, Clawbearer," he said as he reached into his pocket, pulling out his wallet.

"Might I ask why?" I asked as I closed my eyes, tightening my grip on Lees's shoulder as Lees bent down. I could feel Coda shifting, as well, struggling to keep his balance.

"No, you may not," Lees replied, concentrating on working the lock. He had a pair of lock picks in the seams of his wallet. He did not intend to tell an officer from his ship that he had the items; otherwise, they would be obligated to tell him to give them up for the rest of the voyage. It might even result in disciplinary action when, really, he just kept them around because he liked to play with them. With a final giggle of his lock picks, he gently pushed the door open. If I didn't see them, and he didn't tell me about them, I could pretend I didn't know about them.

What we found was slightly surprising: a small room with various supply cargo boxes. All of them were in pretty rough condition. Most of them looked like they would fail inspection. There was one exception, though: a cargo crate of grain that looked like it had been freshly harvested. The crate itself looked new, as well, and it didn't bear the same logos as the rest of them.

We had found Coda's grain from Crown. Now for step two in the plan.

To say that step two was logical or legal would be a stretch in both directions. There was nothing logical about it and I had no idea how I let Lees talk me into it. As for the legality of it...yeah, we won't even go there. Instead, let me just explain it to you. We were going to switch out the grains. Taking a pallet jack that Stone had so handily provided, which meant we stole from his store, Lees pushed the cargo crate straight out the store using the loading bays. Coda and I kept watch from the tops of the various stalls as Lees pushed it down the street and towards the police impound.

Here is where the whole plan got shifty. We were going to replace the contaminated grain with the good grain, and then get a message to Brown that he had to insist on a new inspection. That should result in him and the grain being released early enough to make their scheduled deliveries. Sounded simple, but it was anything but in reality. After all, there was such a thing as cameras.

Getting the grain from Stone's store to the police impound was uneventful. It was a lot of hard work on Lees's part, considering the gaylord weighed almost a thousand pounds, but the handcart was good and it moved the load efficiently. I was surprised I didn't hear any alarms coming from Stone's shop, but I guess he must have thought that his reputation was enough to protect him from theft. Once we got to the impound, the work began.

First, we had to locate and disable the cameras. To do that, Coda and I scouted from the tops of the surrounding partitions, identifying several cameras. Using the type of physics that only cats could employ, we managed to sweep under their lines of sight and disconnect the wires. Humans:

they thought they were the only ones smart enough to handle technology, and therefore didn't design it with their animal companions' abilities in mind.

Next, we had to break into the impound lot. It was a simple square surrounded by a wire fence on three sides, and the police station on the south side. Coda and I made it look easy as we scaled the fence and slipped in through the barbed wire. We had to find the bad grain that Stone had replaced the good grain with and then find a good route for Lees to use to switch out the gaylords. Lees hid behind a partition a block away while we did this. Luckily, dogs weren't the only ones with good noses, and it was only a matter of minutes before we were able to find the bad grain and plan the best route. Lees would have to enter from the north end, cutting through the fence using the bolt cutters that we also borrowed from Stone when we...liberated...the handcart.

Cutting an opening large enough to slip through was more work than we anticipated. The bolt cutters worked, but every cut took a lot of effort from Lees. We should have grabbed the hand torch, but hindsight is twenty-twenty. The wire fencing was reinforced and resisted our efforts. In addition, Lees had to cut an L-shape into the fence, part of it along the top, and then down a side so he could push the crate through. Thankfully, the fence was not secured on the bottom, just along the top and sides. They obviously hadn't had problems with the population breaking in before. Luckily, Lees was strong and determined, so while it took longer than expected, it was still achievable.

Once he pushed the gaylord through, he followed us to the original contaminated grain location. That was when all hell broke loose. You see, we did not know that we had been followed. Remember me saying that I was surprised that there were no alarms at Stone's shop? Apparently there was a silent alarm, one that did not go to the police, but rather to Stone and his goons. They had somehow managed to follow us from their shop to the impound lot, surrounding us right as we got to the other gaylord of grain.

"Now, what do we have here?" one of the goons remarked to the others. I looked over to Coda to see if he recognized them, but he just stood there trembling. Maybe this was Stone? He certainly appeared to be in charge.

"I don't know, boss. What do we have?" another one of them answered. He didn't seem to be the brightest bulb.

"Tommy, shut up. Boys, it appears that we have a couple of thieves. It looks like they stole my grain. Luckily, we're here to get it back. It also looks like they've led us right to our original grain. Looks like we'll be taking that back, too," Stone said. I'm going with him being Stone since the other called him "boss." Why he would follow us into the impound lot was beyond me, since there was always a chance of being caught, but maybe like us, he planned on not getting caught.

"If you knew what this is, why did you ask?" Tommy asked Stone. He looked very confused, and he waved around a flashlight as he spoke. The beam from that flashlight had to be attracting some notice.

"It was a rhetorical question, you nitwit," Stone answered, clearly frustrated. He was also getting loud, confident that they would get away with whatever they were planning.

"We're not thieves! We're simply taking what we paid for and you stole from us!" Coda shouted back at Stone.

"Sorry, kitten, but your captain knew better than to buy from anyone else but me. We had an understanding. In a way, this was your fault. You're the one who insisted that the grain was no good. If he'd had just taken it when he had the chance, you guys would already be on your way and halfway to wherever you were going." Stone sneered in Coda's direction.

"You can't force people to buy from you, and you can't go stealing from others to line your own pockets. You certainly can't steal from Brown and me and get away with it," Coda spat back. They were both getting very loud. Pretty soon, everyone would get caught.

"I can do whatever I want," Stone snapped back.

"FREEZE! POLICE!" came the shout that I had been waiting for.

The impound lights snapped on in all of their blinding glory, lighting up an already well-lit space. Various police vehicles drove up, blocking the narrow walk lanes, and what room was not blocked by the vehicles was blocked by men and dogs in riot gear. They were not playing around. Coda, Lees, and I froze. Stone and his group tried to run for it.

The police dogs that hit them as they ran were a sight to be seen. They made very quick work of catching the offending party and did it with a ruthlessness that made me give those dogs even more respect than before. I wasn't even sure if Stone made it ten steps before he was taken down. He would certainly need stitches. Once the dogs had them, it was quick work for the police to cuff and secure Stone's gang.

Coda, Lees, and I also found ourselves in restraints, although we were not stupid enough to resist. We were arrested, though, and that was going to be a problem.

❧❧❧❧❧ ❦❦❦❦❦

To say that Captain Kostova was angry was an understatement on par with saying that faster-than-light travel was quick. I had seen him mad before, just never mad at me. I was very much hoping that he would send another one of the officers to get us out, but he had come himself. I did not see what he said or did, but he managed to get Lees and me out of detention in record time. We were barely even booked before he was storming into the precinct and pulling their captain aside for a word. Then we were out and in his loving care.

He didn't look to see if we followed him as he stormed from the police station to the ship. He did not speak or acknowledge us in any way. He did not have to. we would have been absolute idiots to so much as dawdle behind him or do anything to attract his notice. His face was a shade of red that I had read about but never seen, and his breath was far from steady. If rage had an image, it was Captain Kostova, and we deserved it.

Once we got to the ship, we were not dismissed. Instead, he led us directly to his office where we found the ship's mate, Bang, waiting for us. He was going to act as a witness.

"What in the hell were you two thinking?" Kostova bellowed as soon as the door had shut. He had not even waited to get behind his desk, but just spun around in front of us.

We were so screwed.

"It was my fault entirely," I started to say.

"I was thinking that we needed to help," Lees said at the same time. Yeah, that was what we thought, but I was the officer between the two of us. I should have known better and I would take the responsibility.

"It is my fault," I almost growled over at Lees. "I saw a civilian in need, decided to help, and since time was limited, I came up with the plan to switch the grains in the hopes that the subsequent inspection would get Captain Brown out of jail and on his way so he didn't miss his shipment." All of this was really Lees's idea, and I had to have been drugged to agree to it. I would be damned if I was going to blame a private for my actions, though.

"Bullshit it was your idea. If you're going to claim it, though, fine," Kostova answered before Lees could interject. "Seriously though, breaking into a police impound lot was the best idea you could come up with? You didn't think that they would catch you? You're luckier than hell that Stone and his men followed you and then were stupid enough to admit to thieving the original grain and setting Brown up to take the fall. You're even more lucky that I happen to have worked with the police captain. Otherwise, you and Lees would be rotting in that cell for breaking into a police station! Most people try to *break out*!" Kostova was yelling by the time he got to that last part.

I might have been stupid enough to go along with Lees's plan, but I wasn't stupid enough to answer Kostova any more than I already did. Talking my way out of this was not going to happen. I just stood there, looking up at him. I had not known we were that close to being in serious trouble. If the ship had to depart without us, we would have been considered away without leave, no matter that we were not detained willingly. Those were serious charges.

Pinching the bridge of his nose, Kostova fought to bring himself back under control. Several deep breaths later, he managed it. "You two are confined to quarters until further notice. The only time you will leave your quarters is to attend to your duties. Meals will be taken in your quarters. There will be no visitors. You both can kiss the next revelry goodbye. Now, get out of my office before I regret not leaving you on Starpath."

He didn't need to tell us twice. We both immediately turned to leave. "Wait, one more thing. You two might as well know that Captain Brown and Coda Paws were both out of the station before you two were. They were able to load the good grain and depart from the dock on time. You were in the wrong and should not have interfered, but you did good all the same. Now get out."

Smothering a smile, we both left, and we quickly. It wasn't until we got to the hallway that we celebrated. Yes, we might've been in trouble and confined to quarters, but we were able to help Coda and Brown. Kostova would get over it, and if I, Major Moggie Clawbearer, was any judge of character, he would not even put it down on our permanent records. Instead, this would just become one of the many stories that he told in the officer messes to other starship captains.

The Watching Constellation

RHIAIN O'CONNELL

THE SOFT "MROOW" NEARLY made Athani Elba jump out of her skin.

She was supposed to be the only living being on the ship, but she knew what she'd heard: there was a cat somewhere on board. Close by, in fact.

Gods, if it's stuck in the loading dock crawlspaces, I'm gonna be pissed, she thought.

"Toroa, are sensors picking up another being on board?" she asked aloud.

"Affirmative," a pleasant female voice responded after a few milliseconds. "Alpha Deck, Corridor 3, Room 2."

"You could've just said 'my stateroom,'" Athani muttered, racing out of the bridge. "On this deck, even. It's not like this rig has a lot of space."

"I am a seventh-generation ship AI," Toroa stated over the ship speaker. "I am programmed to be specific on such details at all times."

Athani rolled her eyes as she stopped in front of her stateroom and toggled the doors open. They obediently slid open with a soft murmur of gears and a flash of silver alloyed smoothness. Despite the size of this bird, her stateroom, her personal and private oasis, was large enough to cancel out any misgivings she'd had in accepting the piloting job.

Curled up on her bed was a black cat with a small white diamond on its forehead. It opened its eyes and yawned widely, then looked up at her, yellow-green eyes slitted.

Athani stared at the feline intruder for a long moment, mouth slightly open. She wiped sweaty palms on her jumpsuit.

The cat "mroow"ed again, and Athani did jump this time.

Where's my food? a voice asked in her head.

❦

She'd been piloting the little boat for almost four standard months before the cat showed up. Before that, Athani had been a shuttle pilot, a liaison between the supply ships that regularly appeared in orbit over Orbve, her homeworld, and the spaceport her parents managed for the provincial government.

It was a sweet gig, but she also knew her parents were trying their best to keep her out of the reach of the visiting pilots who came down for a couple standard days' leave every month. For some reason, they liked to flirt with her—a lot. And she liked to flirt back. She had refused many an offer to warm a pilot's bed at night, and downright cold-shouldered those who offered to pay her for the privilege. No, she just liked to flirt. She was one of those "never been kissed" girls, and didn't mind keeping it that way for a while longer.

If she was honest with herself, she already had a love, and it wasn't bipedal or even a being: she loved flying.

Piloting a shuttle between the spaceport and the supply ships had been her way of seeing Orbve with fresh eyes, and it never failed to delight her that each time she was beyond the ecliptic in the hunkering bulk of shuttle, the view below offered a new perspective on her homeworld. She never tired of watching the mesmerizing swirl of cloud masses that partially hid Freyji, the continent her family lived on, the starkly drawn boundary between night and day as it crossed the horizon, the wink of the stars responding to the wink of the lights in the communities rapidly spreading across Orbve. Catching glimpses of this tableau as she flitted between land and ship was a treasured pearl that she kept close to her heart. When she wasn't in the pilot's seat, she would still come up to help load and offload supplies and visitors as needed.

Athani had transported visitors on the smaller shuttles to the planet surface and the smaller loads of foodstuff and ice on the larger shuttles to the communities that submitted monthly requests in the provincial queues. Her oldest brother, Henry, handled the larger loads and normally piloted their largest shuttle. Her other four siblings helped around the spaceport cleaning, managing traffic, responding to visitor requests and the like.

They hadn't meant to turn the spaceport management enterprise into a family business, but Orbve was still growing, with more beings, mostly human from other near-Earth colonies, immigrating to her world by the hundreds. The provinces predicted seeing a population boom in the thousands in the next decade.

Orbve wasn't exactly a "frontier" planet, but humankind had been expanding into the galaxy for the last six hundred years, and Orbve had seen its first deposit of beings only fifty standard years prior. Each of the five continents was considered a province with its own government, and each province was represented by a being who reported to the planetary government, who reported to the interstellar federation responsible for the planet's settlement in the first place. It was a nice, quiet cycle: predictable, with the human center of civilization decades of light-years away, but humanity had found yet another world to call its own.

Nice and quiet.

Yeah.

She had been transporting visitors to the surface seven months back and had become aware of a man watching her from one of the front seats as she gently set the shuttle down on its usual landing pad. The man had waited patiently as she pressurized the cabin and opened the cabin door so the other beings could disembark. When she had turned around from waving farewell to the last kid trailing after his parent to the main spaceport lounge, he had remained.

"Caft Shoreson," he said, holding out a hand to her, a slight smile on his dark face.

"Athani Elba," she replied, accepting the proffered hand and squeezing his fingers briefly in the usual Orbve way.

Shoreson gestured to the pilot's seat. "You've been doing this awhile," he said.

"Seven years," she confirmed, nodding. "Well, eight in two months. My mom says I'd be bored otherwise."

"You show considerable skill for one so young," he remarked.

Athani couldn't stop the smile that found its way to her face. "Mr. Shoreson, sir, we're a recently settled colony world and I need something to do, or I'd be 'underfoot,' as my dad likes to say when he thinks I'm not in hearing range."

Shoreson outright laughed. "If I understand correctly, your parents manage the provincial spaceport?" At her nod, he said, "I would like to meet them."

It turned out Caft Shoreson was a prominent figure in the Federation government. Her dad had confirmed the stranger's credentials with his contacts at the provincial and planetary levels, but he was taken aback at Shoreson's job offer—for Athani.

"He wants you to fly one of his private ships in the Beta sector," her dad said at dinner that evening. Dalton Elba paused. "I don't understand why he's interested in you, though." At the look on his daughter's face, Dalton said, "Look, sweetheart, you *are* a good pilot, but you've never flown to another system before, much less between systems, and I highly doubt you're familiar with Federation regs that govern all interstellar travel in known space."

"He said the ship has an AI and all I'd have to deal with are in-system flights," Athani countered. She knew why her dad hesitated to give his blessing. Hell, she even understood and agreed with the reasons. Mostly. "Dad, this is the opportunity of a lifetime. I'm not saying I don't want to be a shuttle pilot on Orbve forever, but don't you think some outworld experience would do me some good?"

"I don't know, honey," her dad replied. "I just find it strange that someone like Shoreson would appear out of nowhere to offer you a job."

"It's perfectly understandable," Shoreson said, when father and daughter approached him the next day about their concerns. Okay, Athani's *dad's* concerns. She was feeling more pins and needles about *leaving*. "This would be your daughter's first time offworld, you're concerned about her lack of experience, the appropriate level of training required for this position, and why her?" The dignitary smiled. "I can answer all your questions. I can also put you in touch with other beings from the same age group as Athani whom I've run across in my travels and offered the same job to, and they can give you the what and why."

"Convenient," Dalton Elba said dryly, raising an eyebrow. "Is there a training program? What about compensation and leave?"

The training program lasted for six weeks and would be conducted on the same vessel type Athani would be flying. Much of the training required her to familiarize herself with the ship, its AI, and its capabilities; learn the Federation regs, or at least the relevant bits that regulated her job, specifically; pass the astronavigation modules, as a failure of one meant automatic rejection from the position. One of Shoreson's other young (experienced) pilots would be her trainer. The monthly pay made her dad's eyebrows climb further up his forehead; it was three times more than his monthly provincial stipend as the spaceport manager. Leave was contingent on finishing the training program successfully and completing all in-system flights even *more* successfully in the first six standard months.

It took promising to give him a third of her monthly pay, regular contact, no ifs, ands, or buts, and Shoreson vowing she would be kept safe on his personal honor to get her dad to relent.

"I would not have approached you about your daughter if I did not see any promise in her as the accomplished pilot she will be one day," Shoreson said assuringly, as Athani danced excitedly around her dad's spaceport office. The dignitary paused and held Dalton Elba's gaze. "I promise you will not regret this. Youngsters like Athani are our future."

"I don't know if 'regret' is the correct word so much as 'dread,'" Dalton replied, tone still dry.

"Better to raise an ambassador than a galactic tyrant," Shoreson said, surprising a laugh out of her dad.

Training had been a *breeze*. The pilot who'd trained her was cute and had been flying in Epsilon sector for the last year and a half. He, too, originally hailed from a recently settled colony world, although it took Athani a few standard hours to find his homeworld in their training starmaps.

"Sarkalos is isolated," Goe'e Chithkauz conceded. "And parochial. We are farmers. I didn't want to be a farmer."

Athani inclined her head to one side. "Do you like flying, then?"

The young man's face brightened as he brushed a blonde lock of hair out of his eyes. He wasn't one to leer or grab for her, even in a friendly way, much to her relief. In fact, he was very much a gentleman in his mannerisms and speech. "I *love* flying," he said emphatically. "The only flying vessels we had were used to fertilize the crops, and I took every chance I got to complete that chore." Goe'e lovingly patted one of the control panels on the tiny bridge of their training ship. "Flying my Tiani was an eye-opener, that's for sure."

"Tiani?"

"My ship's AI." Goe'e's smiled broadly.

Athani nodded. "This one is named Toroa." She leaned in and whispered, "I think it has a stick up its you-know-where."

"I am unfamiliar with that euphemism, Athani Elba," the ship AI interjected in her pleasant soprano voice. "My vocabulary library does not include the phrase. I am programmed with limited functions until you successfully complete the training modules and all functions are unlocked."

Athani theatrically rolled her eyes while Goe'e hid his chuckle behind a cough into his hand. "It's not necessarily an insult, Toroa," she said, drawing out the AI's given name. "But you're pretty stiff, for a computer."

The AI didn't respond right away. Then: "I am programmed with limited functions until..."

Athani smacked her forehead with a hand while Goe'e no longer bothered to hide his laughter.

Beta sector was just outside the center of Federation proper—in other words, the core of human-occupied space. Terra and Sol system comprised that core, predictably named Alpha sector, while older members of the Federation rounded out the remainder. Long-established systems and those recently settled further away from the core inhabited the concentric rings of the other sectors that, as predictable as ever, were named after the other letters of the Greek alphabet consecutively.

Athani had been surprised that someone like Shoreson wanted a green pilot to make these flights so close to Terra. She supposed she should feel honored to be flying one of his ships, although the details of her assignment had not been altogether clear until her training had finished.

The disappointment was mild but acute when she learned the "what and why": her Scout-class-but-still-civilian vessel was doing memorial runs in Beta sector. The AI was already preprogrammed with the memorial information of each human-inhabited world and would release it to any watching inhabitants as the ship broke atmo and made an evolution around the planet before flying to the next system and repeating the process. The AI also handled the between-system jumps and necessary comms with passing naval ships, but the actual flying in-system would be done by its human pilot.

Goe'e had had to wait for her to pass training before explaining the details of the assignment. All of Shoreson's pilots were committed to the same project: their vessels released information of the recently passed through the world's comms network. Even his parochial homeworld suffered the same requirement, as it was a clause in Sarkalos's planetary government agreement that allowed it to be a Federation member world.

Humans, unsurprisingly, remembered their dead. Some human worlds seemed fond of remembering their dead loved ones long after it was embarrassingly necessary to pay respects. Shoreson's fleet of memorial ships was his way of allowing all Federation members to pay respects to their dead, economically but whimsically. Athani could've ticked off on her fingers plenty of other avenues in which Shoreson's wealth and amassed influence could be put to good use—besides playing dignitary to current and prospective members of the Federation—but he was her employer now, he paid well, and the job seemed simple, no?

It was also immensely boring. Toroa, the AI with a stick up its ass, turned out to be the AI of *her* ship, ironically named *Chthonia*. Toroa reminded her of a prim and proper governess from eighteenth-century Terran Britain: always correcting her on the nitty-gritty details of a world they were headed to, the programmed memorial release and its layout and length, the nearest constellations, ad nauseum. It was enough to make her clench her teeth and bite her tongue until the AI finally shut up. Toroa had not realized, if it was possible for it to reach this conclusion, that often Athani didn't want its reminders about its many capabilities, or lack thereof. Yet.

The flights themselves were uneventful and quiet. Toroa would announce their arrival in-system. It would provide the local date and time for the memorial release. It would notify Athani when it was time to fly around the world and when it was time to depart. It would inform her of any relevant comms from the world below or passing naval vessels. It didn't bother to tell her she could talk to another human from either place. The one time Athani had asked, Toroa had informed her comms was already complete, the other human was back to whatever business he or she normally conducted, thankyoubutno.

She had asked to see the memorial release itself before they'd arrived in Alpha Centauri, and Toroa had told her she did not have the permissions to view such data. Athani had contacted Shoreson directly (he'd given her his comms info in case she had any problems) and requested access, and upon Shoreson's approval, Toroa had seemed almost reluctant to obey its master, for about two standard seconds—Athani had counted—before allowing her access.

Athani didn't know if one could commit mutiny against an AI, but she'd been close to that point. She didn't know how the ship computer would react to such...tumultuous releases of emotion, but she could certainly provide a demonstration to find out.

There were a few bright points in the humdrum routine Athani reluctantly settled into. The ship contained an almost limitless library and could access every kind of entertainment in existence: vidshows, cybergames, news aggregators, and everything in between. The galley was top of the line, and between the autochef and the stovetop, Athani happily engaged her inner cook to her heart's content.

She could also talk to her family on Orbve whenever she wanted to. Keeping in mind their busy schedule in running the spaceport, she would talk to her dad every evening after dinner to catch up on her siblings' activities and events she'd missed.

It had never occurred to Athani until then that homesickness was, well, a thing.

Then the cat arrived.

The tears came so fast as she tentatively stroked the beautiful creature that Athani started.

"Wh-what's happening?" She quickly scrubbed at her face, but the tears kept falling.

The cat looked up at her. *You're crying,* it said.

"You're *talking,*" she retorted, aware her voice had risen in a wail. "Cats don't talk! Especially in a human's *head!*"

"Athani Elba, is there an issue?" Toroa almost sounded concerned.

"It's Athani, damn you." She realized she was shouting now, but she didn't care. "I keep telling you that, but you never listen! Stop calling me by my full name. It's just *ATHANI!*"

Mercifully, the AI fell silent.

Athani slumped down on her bed next to the cat and leaned against the bulkhead that her bed was pushed up against. She covered her face with both hands, her body shuddering with sobs, the tears still pushing between her closed eyelids and leaking down her cheeks.

She became aware of the cat rubbing against her thigh, its own little body vibrating in a deep resonant purr.

You are sad, it said softly. *You are alone. You miss your family.*

She sniffled and gave a weak laugh. "How are you able to talk to me? In my head, I mean."

You can't understand me if I talk out loud. As if to demonstrate, it released another "mroooow," and no, Athani didn't know what that meant, even if it was deeper and more resolute than the inquisitive "mrooow" she'd first heard over the ship's comms earlier.

"That's true." Athani petted the cat again and was rewarded with another purr as it climbed into her lap. She lifted its hind legs to check its sex, ignoring the indignant yowl. "Do you have a name?"

I am Alex, the cat replied. *And you are Athani.*

Athani smiled despite herself. She hesitated. *Can you hear me?* she thought at him.

I can, but it is still better if we talk in your speech or the funny voice will be worried, Alex replied. *You have a nice voice.*

She laughed. *I might still talk to you like this if I don't want Toroa listening to everything I say.*

"Mweow," Alex said. *Toroa is a computer. She is still trying to understand her pilot.*

Athani sighed. "I don't understand *her.*" She didn't care if Toroa heard her or not. She also belatedly realized she'd just referred to the AI as a "her," as if she was just another being on the ship.

Computers are not supposed to be understood, Alex said primly. *I am hungry, Athani. I need food.*

That was when Athani finally started to feel at home.

⁂

In the following weeks and months, Alex became her shadow. He followed her wherever she went on the ship. He perched on the top of her chair on the bridge, or curled up in her lap while she read a book in her stateroom. Athani fed him small pieces of cooked chicken from the autochef, which became his favorite meal, and it didn't matter what ship's time it was. If he was hungry, he got his chicken.

He refused to tell her how he arrived on the *Chthonia* or how he could communicate mind-to-mind with her. Athani puzzled these things out when she had downtime from her duties. She wasn't sure how to explain the cat's appearance to Shoreson or her family.

Alex introduced himself to both parties eventually. Given that Athani wasn't required to leave the ship or that the *Chthonia* only docked at the scattered orbital stations in Beta sector every few months for supply reloads, the cat's appearance remained a complete mystery to everybody, including Athani.

Toroa, however, seemed to take the feline's presence on the ship in stride. In time, she took over feeding Alex. He would yowl at her frequently, looking up at the ship's ceiling, and Toroa would answer in her pleasant soprano voice, although whenever Athani asked what the cat had said, Toroa would only answer with, "You must ask him directly, Athani."

Athani noted the change in the way the AI addressed her without comment. She still wasn't sure about the computer, but at least Toroa didn't seem to have that stick up her ass anymore.

She was reviewing the memorial address for Ceti Tau when she overheard Alex talking to the AI again, both aloud and in his "mind-voice." Her cat's chattering voice dropped and lifted, weaving together with the words he was apparently allowing her to "hear" in her head.

The vids are boring, Toroa. You should let her make them more exciting.

"The information and graphics are compiled by our employer's assistants at his home office, Alex," the AI replied. "I have no control over how the memorial vids are created."

Do not be disappointed if no one watches them, Alex insisted.

Athani looked up from the screen she was watching and glanced at her cat. "I never gave much thought about how they were created," she said.

Alex's yellow-green eyes gleamed. *You should,* he said with a sniff, his tail straightening into a furry, mostly vertical line in the air. *They are only data reels scrolling across people's screens. Sometimes they interrupt whatever the people are watching and make them angry. How is that a proper way to remember their dead?*

Athani watched her cat thoughtfully, tapping her chin with a forefinger, then slowly reached for the comms controls. "Toroa, is Caft Shoreson currently available for a chat?"

Sometimes it was difficult for her to believe this man had, upon a chance meeting nine months ago, become her employer.

"You are full of surprises, Miss Elba," Shoreson said from the other side of the screen. He wore a bemused expression on his dark face, but Athani didn't see any glimmers of annoyance or disappointment.

"I'm bored, sir," she replied. "Alex keeps me plenty entertained nowadays, and if anybody deserves credit for the idea, it's him."

Shoreson cocked his head to one side, eyebrow raised. While he had accepted the presence of the cat onboard with only a couple questions, Athani could tell he hadn't believed her when she said Alex could talk. "If he wanted a reward for his contribution," the dignitary said, "what would you suggest?"

Alex chose that moment to leap onto her shoulder, startling Athani. His mind-voice again weaved through his audible chatter. *I would like him to remember us in the stars,* the cat said.

Shoreson was staring at the feline. For that matter, so was Athani.

"How do you propose we remember your kind, Master Alex?" Shoreson asked. Athani noted the man's expression was now serious. In fact, it bordered on reverent.

"Wait," Athani said. "Can you *hear* him?"

Shoreson nodded slowly, and tapped his temple. "In here."

Athani looked at her cat. "You can talk to all humans like that?"

Of course I can, Alex said smugly. The cat was looking directly at Shoreson. *Include the people's pets in the memorial vids.*

Shoreson opened his mouth, then closed it.

"That would..." Athani glanced quickly at her employer. "That would take more coordination with each world to gather the necessay data, but it's doable."

"I can contact them," Toroa cut in. "I can also provide them our requirements for the data needed for the memorial releases." The AI paused.
"Please provide those requirements and I will reach out to Ceti Tau prior
to our arrival in-system."

"Done," Shoreson said. The man bowed his head respectfully at Alex,
then focused on Athani. "If this works out, Miss Elba, expect your monthly paycheck to increase."

"Thank you, sir," she said. Her six-month review had been positive, and
there had already been a noticeable bump in her pay, but this was all to the
good if it increased again.

You humans are a creative bunch, Alex remarked after Shoreson signed
off. He jumped off Athani's shoulder and pranced out of the bridge, the tip
of his tail waving in the air. *Sometimes you need a push in the right direction.*

"I suppose we do," Athani said, smiling ruefully. "We just get that push
from the least expected sources."

Alex sniffed and looked over his shoulder at her. *That is why I am here,*
he said, and Athani had never heard her cat sound so serious as he did then.
To remind you.

"Remind me of what?" she asked, but Alex didn't answer.

❧ ⟫⟫⟫⟫ ⟪⟪⟪⟪ ☙

Shoreson certainly employed resourceful people. Between Toroa and
Shoreson's staff, the Ceti Tau memorial release was significantly revised
after they received the additional data requested from the appropriate
planetside officials. If Ceti Tau was confused by the kind of data requested,
they never let on.

Athani pulled up the release as it slowly began to roll across her screen.
She had to focus on the flight as the *Chthonia* made its evolution around
the planet, but she still managed to steal glances at the vid.

Shoreson's staff had outdone themselves. What had once been a silent scroll of photos, with names and dates appearing on the bottom of each picture, was now a dramatic show, including an introduction that explained the purpose of the release and an ending with credits. And the music! Athani wondered if one of the office staff had dug into Terra's history archives for the background instrumental, which was solemn, but not so solemn to induce tears, yet still sorrowful enough to emphasize its serious nature.

Interspersed with the photos of humans were pictures of animals: not just cats, but also dogs, the smaller critters like guinea pigs that children were fond of, even the occasional exotic like a snake and even a cow. Each pet also had their names, dates of birth, and dates of passing included with their photos.

When the initial roll of release ended, it immediately began again as the *Chthonia* streaked across Ceti Tau's blue skies.

❧❧❧❧❧ ❧❧❧❧❧

"Ceti Tau officials report forty-four million viewers," Toroa said.

Shoreson had called her this time. He held up a glass containing an amber liquid and toasted her—and Alex, who was once again perched on Athani's shoulder. "That was brilliant," he said.

Athani smiled. "You know whom to thank, sir." She looked at Alex, who simply "mrooow"ed authoritively, and perhaps a bit too smugly.

Shoreson laughed, but then his expression turned serious as he turned his full attention to the cat. "You have my complete gratitude, Master Alex," he said. "I hope someday you answer our questions about your origins, and how you know so much about, well, this endeavor." The dignitary hesitated. "You do seem to be knowledgeable about many things."

Alex opened his mouth partially, but no sound emerged, nor did Athani "hear" his mind-voice. Then he jumped off her shoulder and trotted out of sight.

Shoreson raised an eyebrow, looking nonplussed, but Athani shrugged. "I will confess, sir," she said. "I didn't have pets growing up, although I know some of our neighbors owned cats. Doesn't mean I understand cats any better now."

Her employer chuckled. "I suspect they keep us deliberately in the dark, Miss Elba."

We do, Alex said, when she walked into her stateroom after ending the call.

Athani jumped. "Could you please stop doing that?" she said crossly. "You do what?"

Keep you in the dark. The lights were dim in the room, but she could still see the glow of his eyes from where he sat on her bed.

Athani began to feel goosebumps on her arms, although she wasn't sure why. "Why do you keep us in the dark?" she asked, sitting down next to him and slowly stroking his fur.

His signature deep purr resonated under her hand, but his mind-voice held a tinge of amusement when he answered. *We like to keep you humans on your toes, but we do not try to get too close to you.*

Athani gathered him up in her arms as she laid down on the bed, re-arranging his protesting little body on her stomach. "You're speaking in riddles," she said. "I'm just a ship pilot doing a job. I'm not...into the mystical stuff, and what you're saying sounds like you're speaking to me from the atmo or something, through a break in the clouds."

Alex looked at her intently. *I was born thousands of years ago, Athani,* he said softly. *I was once just a cat on Terra. When I died, I was transformed into a watcher among the stars. There are many like me who observe you and your kind. We watch you as you are born, and as you die. We are always watching.*

Athani lifted her head and stared at him, her hand stopping midstroke. The goosebumps had turned into chilly streaks running up her back and through her stomach. "Why me?" she finally asked. "I already told you what I am. I'm no one special. I mean," she added hastily, beginning to pet him again, "you've made this job more bearable by being here, don't get me wrong. But I'd imagine there's some other being out there whom you could keep company." She laid her head back down and sighed. "I'm not trying to offend or anything, just...understand."

Alex rubbed his cheek against her fingers, still purring. *I like you,* he said simply. *You were lonely and bored and uninspired. I came here to provide company, abolish your boredom, and inspire you. Is that not enough?*

She laughed and hugged him gently to her. "For now," she answered.

For a long time yet, it was.

What Rory Learned

Z. M. RENICK

Marc Delany slowly opened his eyes and was greeted with a sight out of a horror movie: squirming white tentacles surrounding a great pink maw that was home to four dagger-like yellow teeth. Two great red eyes bulged over it all. Marc did what any human would do upon being confronted with something like this: he let out a blood-curdling scream and leaped out of his bed, scurrying to the other side of the room. It was only then that he got a good look at what had frightened him, and his scream turned to a roar of outrage.

"Rory! I thought I told you to keep your pet under control!"

The subject of this rant sauntered into the room, twitching her tail in a way that made it clear that she was merely humoring Marc by listening to his complaints. She licked her left front paw in an unconcerned fashion, using it to clean her grey fur, then jumped up on the bed, which sagged slightly under her weight. She fixed Marc with her golden-eyed stare and sent her reply directly into his mind. *What has you all in a fit this morning?*

"That!" Marc pointed to his bedside table, where a small white mouse was twitching its whiskers—whiskers that had looked like tentacles when Marc had seen them magnified by the water glass that he kept by his bed at night.

All this fuss over a mouse?

Now that Marc was fully awake, he realized that Rory had a point. The mouse, as frightening as it had looked under magnification, was just a mouse. Still, it was the principle of the thing. A man ought not get pushed around by his cat, even if it was a cat larger than many small dogs.

He switched tactics. "When I told you that you could keep that mouse as a pet, the agreement was that you would control it. You shouldn't be letting it out of its cage."

I didn't. Squeaker let himself out, using his powers.

As if he had asked for a demonstration of those powers, the water glass next to the mouse started to levitate ever so slightly. Marc snatched it out of the air and put it back on the table. "I know what his powers are, but see what I just said about *controlling* him."

He wasn't doing any harm. Besides, we'd need to take him out in another minute, anyway. You're about to be called to work.

"How—" Marc began, but before he got any further, his phone rang. He looked at the number. *Chi Department headquarters.* He groaned internally before answering. "Delany here."

"Agent Delany, we have a Code Five-Oh-Seven at coordinates three-nine-point-one-four, seven-seven-point-eight-five. You've been assigned to assist. Be there ASAP."

"Sir—" But his boss had hung up while Marc's half-asleep brain was still trying to remember what a Code Five-Oh-Seven was or exactly where those coordinates were. Marc sighed and turned to Rory. "You were right, girl. As you always are. Looks like I've got to get to work."

Rory nodded and made her way over to the bedside table, where Squeaker jumped on her back. *We're ready to go when you are.*

"The boss didn't say I could bring you— Eh, he'll deal. Let me get showered and dressed, and we'll head out in fifteen minutes or so." Given their abilities, it was much safer to bring Rory and Squeaker where they wanted to go than it would be to leave them behind. Besides, Marc liked having them with him. He might complain about them sometimes, but the three of them were family: a perfectly ordinary telepathic cat, her perfectly ordinary telekinetic pet mouse, and the tech worker for a top-secret government agency who owned them both—or perhaps who was owned by them both. Some days, it was hard to tell.

Rory and Squeaker were creations of the biologists who worked with Marc's agency. Squeaker had been born because the higher-ups, for some reason known only to them and God, had decided that it was a good idea to splice the alien DNA recovered from the Twin Falls incident into mice, while Rory and her kind had been bred in order to keep the mice under control. Marc had adopted Rory after her project had been canceled, and then she had rescued Squeaker after he'd escaped from his still-active project. And yes, the alien-mouse hybrids were still being bred after the alien-cat project that was supposed to control them had been cancelled, which was the kind of big-picture thinking that the higher-ups were known for.

It was a long drive to the site to which Marc had been summoned. Marc tried to make conversation, but Rory suggested that telepathic communication would distract him from the road, so he just turned on the local classical station. Rory had made a face, switched the radio to heavy metal, and then turned to stare out the window.

Marc drove his car as far as he could, then called for an ATV to pick him up and take him the rest of the way through the wilderness to the alien spaceship. The Chi Department might refer to these things as "a Five-Oh-Seven" or "an artificial object of assumed extraterrestrial origin," but in his own mind, at least, Marc was going to call a spade a spade and a flying saucer a flying saucer.

The ship was a relatively small one as those things went. From the outside, it looked like a silver sphere about ten feet in diameter. Marc walked up to the scientists who were already there poking it and asked, "So what do we have?"

"Still unknown. Superficially, at least, there are some similarities to what we found in Twin Falls."

Marc nodded. "Well, I'll see what I can get out of the computer. Where do I plug in?"

The other agent looked slightly embarrassed. "We don't have any place for you to plug in. We haven't gotten inside yet."

"What? Wait, why am I even here, then?"

"We wanted you just in case we made it in and needed some computer analysis."

"And for that you dragged me out of bed before dawn?"

The other shrugged. "Sorry. Orders from the guys upstairs."

Marc continued to grumble under his breath. It seemed as though everything in the Chi Department got blamed on the guys upstairs. Granted, nearly everything in the Chi Department was in fact their fault, but the guys upstairs weren't here, and these people were. They made a much more convenient target for his annoyance.

In Marc's arms, Rory twisted and squirmed. Recognizing that she was likely as bored as he was, Marc let her go. She leaped to the ground and landed gracefully on her feet. She looked up at Marc—no, not at Marc, at his left jacket pocket. Squeaker poked his head out of that pocket, twitched his whiskers, then jumped onto Rory's back. Satisfied, she darted off into the long grasses.

Marc called after her, "Look after Squeaker. Don't let him get lost."

One of the agents examining the ship looked up. "Wait, you're asking your *cat* to look after your pet mouse?"

"She likes him. Squeaker is really more her pet than mine."

"Wait, your cat has a pet mouse?"

Marc shrugged and said vaguely. "Cats. Who can understand them?"

Though, truth be told, Marc *did* understand a bit more about the kinship Rory felt with Squeaker. She'd told him once that she and Squeaker were "cousins on the alien side," meaning, he guessed, that the same DNA that had been spliced with the white mouse had also been inserted into her.

Marc watched for a while as the various Chi Department scientists poked at the sphere, took soil samples, and got confused expressions on their faces. Occasionally, he saw a grey tail poking out of the weeds and waving about in various places; it appeared that Rory and Squeaker were conducting their own investigation. As for Marc, he was just bored. His investigations couldn't take place until they discovered whether there was a computer inside this sphere. Until then, all he could do was stare at everyone else. He didn't even have a book or something; he'd assumed he'd be working, so he hadn't thought to bring anything to keep himself entertained. He gave a dramatic sigh.

"Mrow?" came a sympathetic voice from the ground.

Marc leaned down to pick up Rory, who was rubbing up against his ankles. "Yeah. Mrow. That's about how I feel right now. You guys seen all you wanted to see here?"

Rory didn't respond, either verbally or telepathically. She just pressed her head against Marc's neck, and Marc responded by petting her. The feel of her fur beneath his hands and her warm weight in his arms were awfully comforting, enough to make him forget his annoyance at being dragged out into the wilderness at four in the morning, and just enjoy the company of his pet.

Suddenly, Marc stopped and looked around. Only one of his two animals was with him. "Where's Squeaker?"

"Mrow," Rory said innocently.

From in front of them, Marc heard a great grinding sound, like some long disused piece of machinery finally starting up again. A couple of the agents gave a cry, and Marc looked towards the sphere. There was an opening in it now, about two feet wide and eighteen inches high. It wasn't much, but it was enough for people to crawl through if they were skinny enough. A couple of the agents were doing that right now. *Maybe they've finally found something for me to do.* Marc hurried over to the sphere.

On the ground, on the burnt earth next to the ship, was Squeaker. When Marc walked by, the little mouse gave a plaintive cry, sat on his hind legs, and waved his front paws in the air. Marc knelt to pick him up and put the little guy back in his pocket.

Meanwhile, the other agents were buzzing about with excitement. Marc went up to one of them, a young woman with dark hair, and asked, "How did you finally get the ship open?"

"I'm not exactly sure," she said. "Charlie was kind of poking at it when it just suddenly popped open. I guess he must have pressed a switch or something, but I could have sworn that we'd already been over that part of the ship at least a dozen times."

"That's the way it happens sometimes with these things." And it was. Marc had seen it enough during his time with the Chi Department. But given how suddenly the sphere had opened and remembering exactly where he'd found the telekinetic mouse afterwards, Marc had his doubts. He reached into his pocket. "What do you have to say, you little stinker? Did you use your powers to open the ship?" He turned to Rory, sitting at his feet. "And were you deliberately distracting me while he did it? Is that why you suddenly got so affectionate?"

"Queek!" said Squeaker. Rory just gave Marc a look with her big eyes.

"Well, if you did, I guess you did me a favor. If there's something I can look at inside there, this trip won't be a total waste of time. And if there isn't, at least we'll know and can go home, rather than being stuck here waiting."

Another female agent stuck her head out of the sphere and looked about. "Delany!" she called. "There are a lot of machines in here. I think we could probably use your expertise.

Marc went and poked his head inside. "Is there room for me to come in?"

"It's a bit tight, but you should fit. Come on!"

Marc stuck his arms and shoulders through the opening, and with a bit of wiggling, managed to pull himself inside. Hardly gracefully, however; he landed on top of the other agent with an "Oof!" and the two took some time to untangle their limbs in the tight confines of the sphere. Finally, they got themselves sorted out, and Marc got a good look at the inside of the sphere. It was covered in etchings and blinking lights, along with a few pieces that stuck out from the walls at odd angles.

The woman saw Marc looking at those. "My best guess is that they're antennas of some sort. Those were one of the things we hoped you could analyze."

Marc opened his laptop, turned on its sensors, and tried to bring it close to one of the supposed antennas. It was a challenge, having to maneuver around both of the agent's shoulders, and around Rory, who had jumped into the sphere when Marc wasn't looking and was now sitting on the agent's head.

"I think you're right," Marc said at last. "It's receiving something... I feel..." Marc tried to maneuver the laptop to get a better signal and ended up whacking the agent on the back of the neck while at the same time banging his own elbow on something sharp. "Ow! And, er, I'm sorry about that. Do you think you could leave me alone here for a few minutes? I think I might have better luck if there was a bit more room."

She nodded and squirmed her way back out of the opening, Rory jumping off her head as she did so. This analysis would be easier without having to worry about Rory, either, but Marc wasn't so foolish as to try to order *her* to leave if she wanted to stay.

Now that it was just him and his pets in the sphere, it wasn't quite so cramped. It wasn't particularly comfortable, but he had certainly sat on airline seats that were worse. He wouldn't want to fly to California in this space, but he'd be fine for whatever length of time it took to do his job. Marc had room to maneuver now, and he sat down as he moved his laptop next to the antenna. There was a signal coming into it. Most of the alien signals he'd seen were little more than static, but there seemed to be something familiar about this, a pattern he could almost recognize...

A long clang suddenly pulled Marc out of his analysis. He looked behind him, towards the exit. The small gap was closing! Marc gave a cry and tried to turn around and get out, but he couldn't move very fast in the enclosed space. By the time he reached the opening, it was barely big enough to stick his hand out. He started to do just that, but he had no way to stop the hole from closing. All he would do was crush his fingers. He yanked his hand back through just in time. The opening sealed, and Marc was trapped inside the sphere.

Marc took a couple of deep breaths and did his best not to panic. Yes, he was a prisoner in a small alien craft, but several of the Chi Department's best experts in alien technology were right outside. They'd find a way to rescue him. They'd gotten the ship open once, after all. They could do it again. And if they couldn't...

Marc reached into his pocket and pulled out his mouse. "Squeaker, did you open this ship the first time? If so, do you think you could do it again? I...I would be extremely grateful."

Squeaker looked down for a moment, and then closed his red eyes. The sphere shook slightly and then disappeared. Stunned, but grateful, Marc moved to leave, only to strike the side of the sphere. *It hasn't disappeared after all. It just went invisible.* Marc tried not to think about the implications of that. He darted to the side of the sphere and started pounding on it. Outside, a group of agents were talking seriously, but none of them seemed to see Marc. Suddenly, one of them gasped and pointed. *Finally!* But then Marc felt the sphere moving under his feet again, and he realized that they weren't pointing at him. They were getting farther away from him. The sphere was rising into the air!

Marc screamed like a little girl, but there was no one to hear him. *No one except...* Marc looked down at the mouse in his hand. Squeaker's eyes were still closed, and he was so still that for a moment Marc wondered if he'd had a heart attack. He didn't react when Marc poked him. The mouse was still breathing, though much more slowly than a creature that size usually did. *It's almost like he's in a trance. Or maybe...*

Marc looked to the cat on the floor, who seemed remarkably unconcerned by recent developments. "Rory!"

She simply looked at him.

"No, Rory, don't give me the silent treatment now. I need to know: is Squeaker the one who's making this ship float?"

Rory continued to stare at him. Then, at last, she said, *Yes. He's sealed the probe and activated the atmospheric engines.*

The probe? That was interesting information, but it was an issue to be dealt with another time. "Can't you stop him?"

I could. But the ship continued to rise. Apparently, Rory was not making use of her ability to stop the mouse.

Marc tried to tell himself that it was because they were too high. If Rory simply forced Squeaker to shut down the engines, all three of them would plunge to the ground and almost certainly die. Surely Rory could convince Squeaker to slow the engines and slowly lower them back to Earth, couldn't she? They were rapidly moving to the top of the troposphere, and Marc could see outer space starting to surround them. "How are we going to get down?"

We aren't.

Marc gaped at Rory, unable to comprehend what she was saying. She left her spot at his feet and went to the edge of the sphere, resting her paws against the invisible wall. The part of the wall she was touching suddenly became visible again, showing visible blue and purple lights. Rory tapped her paws a couple of times against those lights.

"Rory, what are you doing?"

Searching.

"For what?"

For my kin. The rightful owners of this probe.

Her kin... Marc remembered what he'd been told when he'd first arrived: that this ship was similar to the one that the Chi Department had found in Twin Falls. *I'm pretty sure that the alien DNA that created Squeaker—and Rory—also came from Twin Falls.*

Rory gave a yowl that sounded triumphant to Marc's ears. She moved to a different area of the sphere, which likewise became visible at her touch. She again pressed a couple of different lights, and this time, the sphere started to spin. Marc staggered backwards, striking his head against the edge of the sphere. Before he could try to stand up, he found himself thrown to the other side of the sphere by an incredible force. He felt the pressing against every part of his body as his face was smashed against the wall, almost crushing him, making it feel like he was going to be smashed to atoms...

And then the pressure was gone. Marc took a deep breath and rolled over, trying to recover from what had just happened. He felt gentle pads on his shoulder. He turned to see Rory looking concerned.

I'm sorry. It took me a couple of tries to engage the inertia dampers. Are you okay?

Marc gingerly shook out his arms and examined his legs. "I don't think there's anything broken." He touched the back of his head and felt a bit of blood. "I've got a slight cut back there. I hit my head pretty good."

I'm sorry about that. I didn't mean it. I was just so excited to get to them.

"Them?" Marc asked, then shook himself. It was a stupid question. Rory had already told him who "they" were: the aliens who had built the sphere, the ones who had crashed in Twin Falls, the ones who had contributed their DNA to Rory and Squeaker.

Rory nodded. *They're currently in orbit around Io.*

"Io? As in, Jupiter's moon, Io?"

That's the only Io I know of in this system.

Io. Great. He had thought that the sphere was too tight for a trip to California, and now he was flying to Jupiter in it. Of course, the *flying* to

Jupiter was probably better than how the trip would end. "Rory? What are you going to do when we find them?"

Give them back their probe along with the data it collected. And then go home.

"And by home, you mean back to Earth, right?" But Marc knew she didn't.

No. Back with my family. To my real home.

"Rory, Earth *is* your real home. With me and Squeaker."

Squeaker agrees with me on this. We both want to find our real families.

"Nothing I've heard about these aliens suggest that they're nice. This isn't a good idea."

I've spent my whole life on a planet ruled by those who aren't nice.

"That's not fair. I've always been good to you, haven't I? For God's sake, Rory, I saved your life! And Squeaker's!"

You saved us after other humans threatened to kill us for no reason.

Marc couldn't deny that one, unfortunately. "Not everybody is the Chi Department or the Guys Upstairs. There are good humans."

And I'm sure there will continue to be. They just won't be around us.

Us. Marc asked, "What about me? What happens to me when you and Squeaker go home?"

Rory seemed slightly sad when he next heard her in his thoughts. *I'm sorry about that, too. It seemed like there was always going to be someone in the sphere. It didn't feel like Squeaker and I could get in there alone. Us along with you was the best we could do.* She brightened. *Don't worry. It'll be okay. I won't let them hurt you. You were good to me when I was your pet. I'll be good to you now that you're mine.*

Marc tried to imagine life sleeping on a giant pillow under Rory's desk while occasionally being fed seafood delicacies. *I've got to admit it doesn't sound that bad,* a part of him admitted, and he immediately scolded that part for being far too willing to sell out his dignity. But in addition to the humiliation he would suffer, there was another problem: he was pretty sure that Rory was kidding herself about the aliens and their likely welcome among them.

"Rory, you don't know how these guys are going to react to you. You've got some connection to them, but mostly, you're a cat. From what I've heard, these guys aren't exactly animal lovers."

From what you've heard? And just who did you hear it from? Those "guys upstairs" that you're always disparaging? Do you really think they know anything?

"No, but—" Marc tried to issue a few more protests, but Rory was implacable. Eventually, she stopped responding to his entreaties—and eventually, he stopped issuing them.

Space rushed by, and Marc looked at the bleak emptiness outside his window. Intellectually, he'd always known that space was mostly just, well, space: a vacuum with a few tiny specks of matter at vast distances from each other. But he'd always imagined a trip to space being a whirlwind tour of planets, moons and asteroids. The simple blackness was enough to unsettle him, even without his other fears.

In front of them was a star that looked red to Marc's eyes, and eventually, he realized that it was their destination. The star grew closer and closer, and sooner than Marc would have thought possible, it started to take shape. First, Marc started to see white among the red, and then the colors resolved themselves into stripes. Marc could see them spinning in clearly defined layers, with the exception of a single, eye-shaped red splotch that moved about the layers and distorted everything near it. *The great red spot,* he realized. *We're here. Jupiter, the King of the planets. Millions of miles from earth.*

Rory gave a smug meow. *Five hundred million miles, the way that you humans measure distance.*

Five hundred million miles... Marc tried to do the math, figuring out how fast they could have accelerated without killing themselves, and at that rate, how quickly they could have traveled the distance. *It's impossible.*

We'd have been turned into paste. Even with the most generous assumptions, a journey to Jupiter would be a matter of days, not hours; Marc wasn't sure exactly how much time had passed since they'd left Earth, but he wasn't hungry yet, so his stomach could be certain that it hadn't been *that* long.

Impossible for your people. Not for mine. Rory was definitely smug now. She went back to some of the visible lights and started pressing buttons again. The sphere turned, and rather than facing the great planet, they now headed for one of the moons, one that appeared yellow.

As they continued their journey, Rory continued to talk. *Just imagine what you're going to learn. You've always liked science, haven't you? You're about to discover areas of science that you never even knew existed. Ways of manipulating energy that you never thought possible, chemical bonds such as you've never seen on Earth, biology that—*

Rory's thought cut off so suddenly that it left Marc with a throbbing pain in his temple. He'd never experienced anything like it: something in his own mind, a thought like one of his own that just stopped with no warning. It was almost like being knocked unconscious. Only he wasn't the one in trouble.

"Rory!" he cried.

Squeaker squiggled out of Marc's pocket and scampered over to where Rory was still leaning against the lighted panel. "Queek?"

I'm all right, both of you. Just let me think.

Squeaker went up to her and put his tiny paw on her face next to her whiskers. She seemed to appreciate the touch and started purring.

After a moment, Rory looked at Marc. *I've decided that you're right.*

"What?"

It's not right for Squeaker and me to kidnap you just because we want to go home. You belong with your own people on Earth. We should take you back to them.

"Queek," Squeaker agreed.

Rory spun the sphere again. This time, Marc had a bit of warning, and with the help of the inertia dampers, was able to keep his feet. But he again felt the incredible force pushing him back. He leaned against the edge of the sphere to avoid being forced into that position. "Rory? Are the inertia dampers working?"

Yes. Mostly. We're just pushing them to their limits. A bit of the force is getting through.

"You're using even more acceleration than you did when we came?"

Yes, obviously. We need to turn around, for starters. And then I'm sure you want to get home soon, don't you?

"I guess so, but we don't need to push it that hard."

We do. We only have a couple of hours before we miss lunch.

"I don't think that missing lunch is worth tearing this ship apart."

I do. So does Squeaker.

Marc gave up. *I might as well just stay along for the ride. That's what I've been doing this whole time.* He wondered what it would be like to have an ordinary pet. A dog who wanted nothing more than to fetch tennis balls, a hamster who would just stuff its cheeks full of nuts, or best of all, a goldfish who would need nothing more than a few flakes sprinkled on the top of the water...

Marc was so intent on his vision of a lower-maintenance pet that, for a moment, he thought he could see those flakes on the water that his simple goldfish would eat. The water was grey. Then he realized that he really was seeing flakes in front of his eyes, and the grey was Rory's fur as she climbed on his chest.

Marc? Are you okay?

Marc couldn't remember Rory every using his name before. "Iz okay..." he started to say. And then the flakes got much bigger. He couldn't see Rory anymore. It seemed easier to just close his eyes.

When Marc opened his eyes again, he was in an open field. Several people were hovering over him. "Delany? Delany? Are you okay?"

"Rory just asked that," he muttered. He tried to push himself to a sitting position and immediately got dizzy again. He laid back down.

"What happened?"

"Rory..." Marc started to say before his brain fully woke up. "Rory! Where is she?"

"Right here," said one of the other agents. She held up Rory by the armpits, giving Marc a good view of the cat. Squeaker was sitting on her head. Marc chuckled at the sight. *Rory's not going to like that.* For once, though, Rory didn't seem particularly concerned about her dignity.

Marc rolled over onto his side. In front of him, he could see the alien sphere, looking slightly worse for its trip through space and return to Earth. But the weeds in the meadow around him looked much as they had this morning. It seemed that Rory and Squeaker had returned them to the same place from which they left.

"What time is it?" he asked.

"Almost three o'clock," said the agent.

"I guess we missed lunch after all." That was all Marc could think of to say.

The agent responded to Marc's comments. "By most standards, yes, but I think we could still find you something."

Marc's stomach did flip-flops at the thought of food. "Nothing for me, thanks. But you should get something for my cat. She gets cranky when she misses meals."

The agent nodded. "What happened?"

Marc shrugged. He'd had enough time now to clear his brain of most of the fog and think of a story, a good mixture of truth and lies. "I guess

I must have activated something when I tried to read what those sensors were doing. The door suddenly closed, and then the sphere took off."

"We saw the sphere seal itself and then take off. NASA soon lost it on their sensors. How deep into space did it go?"

"I can't be sure. I hit my head almost as soon as things started moving around." The head injury would give him a good excuse for not giving any details about what had happened after they had left Earth. Doubtless, many of them would have been interesting to the Chi Department, but Marc wasn't about to betray Rory, no matter what she had almost done.

"You should probably have that looked at. You may have a concussion."

Marc couldn't disagree. The world seemed to be spinning, and he felt like he was about to throw up.

༄༄༄༄ ༄༄༄༄

Are you sure you're okay? Rory asked again when they finally got home.

"I'm sure. The doctor said it was only a mild concussion, and I don't have any other injuries." The dizziness he'd felt when she suddenly started accelerating back towards Earth hadn't entirely faded, and the fact that he'd lost consciousness during that probably wasn't good for him, either.

I'm so sorry I hurt you. I didn't mean to.

"All is forgiven. I won't say I enjoyed the trip, but I don't think there was any serious harm done. Let's just not do it again, okay?"

Rory nodded. Marc settled into his favorite chair, and Rory leaped into his lap. Squeaker climbed up next to them, making himself a small nest on the right armrest.

Rory said, *Marc? I really am sorry. I promise it will never happen again. Squeaker and I won't try to go to the aliens.*

Marc was a bit curious at that phrasing. *Not "Squeaker and I will never kidnap you again," but a promise that she isn't going to try to go back to the aliens, the people she was calling kin just this morning.* A theory about that came to Marc. "Rory, when we were near Io, did we get close to the alien ship?"

Slowly, Rory nodded.

"By any chance, were we close enough for you to use your telepathic powers on them? What did you sense from them?"

I... Rory let the thought trail off. *I realized you were right. Squeaker and I were wrong. Don't make me admit that again.*

Rory sounded so indignant that Marc couldn't help laughing slightly. "Okay, I promise, Your Majesty. This little error in judgment will be forgotten. Now, come on. Let's all have dinner."

Yet, forgetting wasn't quite that easy. As he laid awake that night, Marc again found himself wondering what Rory had sensed from the aliens that caused her to abandon her plans and run back to Earth at top speed. He knew that he'd spend many dark moments imagining what Rory had learned.

Prides and Prejudice

JOHN VAN STRY

"Why do we have lions onboard the ship?" Harris asked, looking at the crew manifest in shock.

"Piracy," Troy replied.

"What do lions have to do with piracy?"

"They're our security, that's what."

"*Lions*? How in the hell are they our security? All they ever do is sleep!"

Troy sighed. "That's the point."

"Oh? So what happens if we do get hit by pirates? They're going to be speed bumps on the floor or something?"

"Have you ever even *met* any of our lions?"

"No, of course not!"

Troy snorted again. "Typical."

"What's that supposed to mean?" Harris said, frowning at him.

"It means that maybe you should meet them before you start running your mouth. Seriously. Were you like this on your last assignment?"

"We didn't have any lions or other animals onboard my last ship."

"Yeah, well, don't let the captain hear you calling them 'animals.' Besides, why should you care? You don't have to deal with them. You're the purser."

"That's the problem! I have to make sure we've got enough food, water, and recycling capability for everyone onboard, and there's how many of those freeloaders onboard?"

"Fifteen."

"Right! Fifteen lions who do nothing but sleep all day! And what are the odds we'll get attacked, or even boarded? Hell! Why don't we just have some regular marines? At least they don't sleep all day!"

"The reason why we have lions instead of marines is that very reason you're complaining," Troy said wondering if Harris would be here any longer than it took the captain to find a replacement. "Lions sleep twenty hours a day—"

"Yeah! That's what I'm complaining about!"

"Whereas your average marine sleeps what, six? Eight?"

"Exactly! They're not lazy!"

"Yeah, and they eat three meals a day, generate waste for each of those meals and consume oxygen and all of those other resources for sixteen to eighteen hours a day. While our lions eat *one* meal a day, generate far less waste because of that, and as they're sleeping the other twenty, they're consuming less oxygen, water, and all those other resources. For the price of *one* of your marines, we get *four* lions."

"Okay, so we get more. They're still not marines!"

Troy just shook his head. "You'll see."

"What's that supposed to mean?"

"It means we're going to be underway for six weeks, and as one of the three prides is awake for half of each eight-hour watch, unless you're really good at hiding, sooner or later you'll get to meet all of them."

"What! They have free run of the ship?" Harris said, looking shocked.

"They're ship's security, what did you expect? How long have you been in space, anyway?"

"Eight years."

"And you've never flown on a ship with a genner before?"

"The union doesn't allow any of those animal freaks onboard the system haulers!"

Troy just shook his head; the folks in the Sirius system obviously had a few biases. He could only guess the reason as to why Harris had been hired on.

"I need to get up to the bridge. Do you have any last-minute requests or issues that I need to tell the captain before we pull out?"

"No, everything is fine. I've already entered my final stores report into the system."

"And everything is stowed and ready to get underway?"

"Yes, of course it is."

"Thanks," Troy said, checking his tablet and updating the ship's status. That done, he headed up to the bridge. He debated whether to tell the captain about Harris's attitude, but suspected that the captain had more important things to worry about.

Harris shook his head in disbelief as the second mate headed up to the bridge. He couldn't believe they had animals on the ship! Seriously, what were these people thinking?

Going back to his desk, he sat down and ran through all of his spreadsheets one last time to be sure he hadn't missed anything. The alert window on his console was counting down to push-back, and it was always wise, he'd found, to take one last look. Canceling or delaying push-back was a lot cheaper than having to pay some local station hauler to bring something out to them. It wouldn't be the first time he'd gotten a "last-minute request" from someone who decided to check their stores *after* the ship had been cleared to leave rather than before.

Thankfully, that didn't happen this time. It did appear that Captain Curtis ran a tight ship. The *Silver Comet* was a rather large freighter, the largest that Harris had ever been on, but then they went up and out into deep space and hauled from system to system, where it only became economically feasible if you hauled truly massive amounts of cargo on each trip.

He hadn't wanted to take this job, and if he'd known he'd be shipping with animals—fifteen of them, no less!—he just might not have taken it. But he needed the money, and they'd been more than willing to advance half of his income for the trip so he could pay off his wife's medical bills. He sighed at that, for probably the hundredth time. At least *this* time, he'd checked on the medical benefits. Hampton Freightways was far more generous than his previous employer, and didn't balk on technicalities.

Putting all of that out of his mind, he went over the numbers for this voyage and checked over his estimates and compared them to the ones that the company had provided as the normal usage markers for the ship and the crew.

The crew was actually quite small, consisting of the captain, plus four mates, two stewards, one cook, four deckhands, and four engineers, one of which was the chief engineer. Adding him to that, it was seventeen, plus the fifteen "security" forces.

At over a quarter million tons fully loaded, the *Silver Comet* was far larger than anything he'd sailed on before. The ship was absolutely gigantic. At some point, he'd have to go inspect the cargo, which would mean transversing the length and width of the cargo holds. While not a lot could happen to cargo on a ship this size, he'd gotten into the habit of checking it, if for no other reason than it would help stave off the boredom a long trip could bring. And at six weeks, this would be the longest trip he'd ever been on.

❧❦

Two weeks had gone by, and Harris had counted himself fortunate that he had *yet* to run into any of the "animals" onboard. He'd simply checked the schedule for when they would be "awake" and just made sure he either stayed in his bunk or in his office during those times.

So it came as some surprise to him, as he was sitting in the mess eating his lunch, when a feminine voice asked, "Is this seat taken?"

"No," he said, more out of surprise than anything else as a *lioness* sat down beside him at the table. He couldn't help but stare. The first thing he noticed was that she was *big*! Easily as big as he was, maybe even a little bigger. She was covered in tawny-colored fur, or at least the parts of her he could see were, as she was wearing body armor over a ship's jumpsuit that had a fair bit of gear attached to it, with a helmet of some sort hanging off her right hip.

Her head looked very much like that of a lion's, or lioness's, that was. Her muzzle was perhaps a bit shorter, more human-like in some ways, and as she set her tray of food on the table, he noticed that her hands were also covered in fur. He didn't see any fingernails.

"Hi, I'm Cassy," she said with a smile that was only slightly intimidating, as he could see that she definitely had a healthy set of fangs in her mouth.

"Harris..." he stammered as he stared at her.

"Never seen a lioness before, have ya'?" she said with a wink, and then turned to her food.

"Na...no," he said, and watched as she started cutting into one of the steaks on her plate with her silverware.

"Well, I haven't seen you around here before. You're our new purser, aren't you?"

"What? Yes! How'd you know?" he asked, a bit concerned that she seemed to know who he was.

"Ship's security. We have to know who the crew is, where they work, where they bunk, all of that. In case of an emergency."

"I thought you didn't get up until sixteen hundred?" he asked, still unable to take his eyes off her. She was sitting *right next to him*!

"Oh, that's Todd's pride. I'm in Sherman's. We pull an eight-hour shift whenever engineering does an inspection."

"What? Why?"

"'Cause we're all rated as engineering techs in our pride," she said with a shrug of her shoulders.

"It cuts down on costs," another lioness said, sitting down on the other side of him. Her nametag identified her as Anna. "A ship this big really needs twice as many engineering techs as it's got. But we're all cross-trained, so if they need us, we're here."

"Bu... But I thought you all had to sleep for twenty hours a day!" he blurted.

"Only if there's not much else to do," Cassy said with a shrug of her shoulder. "I mean, shipboard life gets kinda boring. So we sleep..."

"Or do *other* things," Anna said with a wink and a leer at him.

"Hey, who's our new friend?" a much deeper voice asked.

Looking up, it was all Harris could do to keep from bolting out of his seat. Standing on the other side of the table with a tray piled almost to overflowing with meat was a *lion*. If he'd thought the girls were big, he was *huge*! There were two more lionesses with him, one to either side, and he was at least a foot taller than they were, and where they didn't have any hair on their heads like the other two, the lion, Sherman, according to his nametag, most definitely had a mane.

"Oh, this is Harris, the new purser," Cassy said. "Harris, this is Sherman, our husband and mate."

"Our?" Harris said.

"They're my pride," Sherman said, sitting down as the other two lionesses joined them.

"I don't think he's ever seen lions before," Cassy added by way of explanation.

"Oh," Sherman said with a shrug. "Well, I hope we didn't upset you or anything. I've been told we're a bit much when we've got all of our weapons on and all that. Unfortunately, as ship security the regs require us to go armed whenever we're on duty."

"Oh...umm... Oh, look at the time. I'm sorry, I need to get back to my office," Harris said, and getting up, he quickly walked away, leaving the mess without a backwards glance.

"I guess Troy was right," Tracy, one of Sherman's other wives, said. "He really doesn't like us."

"At least he didn't piss himself," Anna laughed. "He was almost terrified."

Sherman shook his head and sighed. "Did you *have* to sit down next to him, Cassy?"

"'Course I did!" Cassy said, with a hint of a purr. "I wanted his desssert!"

Grinning, she snagged the untouched dessert off the tray Harris had left behind.

Harris was panting by the time he got back to his office. They looked almost human! He couldn't believe it! He had *thought* that the animals would at least look like...like *animals*!

"Hey, Harris, you doing okay?" Troy asked, stepping into his small office.

"Huh? What?" Harris said, looking up.

"You ran by me in the passageway. Was worried that something might be wrong."

"I was in the mess when...I thought you said they were lions!"

Troy had to fight to keep the smirk off his face as he replied. "I thought that'd be obvious from... Wait! You thought that we had *lion* lions? A bunch of four-legged beasts?"

"Of course! What else was I to think?"

"Haven't you ever seen one of the genetically modified species before?"

"Of course not! We don't have such things out in Sirius! Why didn't you tell me that they were shaped like real people?"

Troy stood with his arms crossed, one hand scratching at his chin.

"I don't know if I'd say they look like regular people there, Harris. I mean, they're way the hell bigger than I am. Plus, they don't have any hair and are covered in fur with tails," he said slowly.

"They walk upright and have hands and all that!"

"Well, yeah, it'd be kinda hard for them to use regular weapons or tools if all they had were paws, now, wouldn't it?" Troy drawled slowly, still looking like he was deep in thought.

"And that's another thing! They're actually working in *engineering*?"

"Oh, only when we're short-handed."

"You're okay with them entrusting the safety of this ship to a bunch of animals?" Harris said, wide-eyed in disbelief.

"Um, you did notice that they're all armed? With pistols and rifles?"

"Anyone can use a gun! But our lives depend on those systems in engineering!"

"Oh, I'm sure Nelson down in engineering would intervene if it looked like they were gonna break something."

"How can you be so calm about this?"

Troy shrugged. "'Cause I've been shipping with them for the last three years? Seriously, Harris, you need to give that line of thinking a rest. Do you really think our bosses would risk a two hundred million standard-cred ship with an untrained and unreliable crew?"

"Well, I don't like it!" Harris grumbled.

"It's not about what you like or what I like. It's about what the accountants like. And the accountants like crewmembers whom they can pay less, and who can do double-duty and they don't have to find work for on these long trips between systems. *That's* what they care about. That's why we've got Sherman and the rest onboard: because it's cheaper than hiring humans, assuming we can even *find* any humans to take the job!"

"What? There are plenty of humans who want these jobs!"

"Oh? Captain told me that you were the only one who *applied* after we lost Stephanie! Which reminds me, just *why* did you sign on? Guy like you, I'd suspect, likes going home on the weekends."

"My wife has a rare form of cancer and the operation to treat it wasn't covered by my previous employer's insurance. Hampton Freightways said if I do two years with them, they'll cover it."

"Two years? That must be some pretty expensive surgery."

"It is."

"Damn, that sucks. Sorry to hear it. Must be rough on her, you're being away while she's sick."

"They put her in a medical suspend unit. They had to. She doesn't have much longer to live. *That's* why I took this job! I had to leave our kids with her parents because I won't be back for at least a year."

Troy sighed and felt like a heel.

"I'll let the Sherman and the others know to give you a wide berth and not talk to you. But if you want some free advice?"

"Sure, why not?" Harris said.

"Stop worrying about them. Just treat them like people and ignore the physical differences. It'll make your life a lot less stressful."

"But they're not human," Harris said in a softer voice.

"They're not as different as you think. Humans raised them, humans trained them. Worse comes to worse, just close your eyes and pretend you're talking to a human."

"But I'm not!"

"Well, if you want to keep your job, I suggest you start pretending they are," Troy said with a heavy sigh. "Look, once everyone hears why you're here, no one is going to want to cost you your job, okay? No one is going to go out of their way to cause issues. I'm sure everyone will look the other way as much as possible. But if push comes to shove, it won't go well for you. So just close your eyes, think of your wife's surgery and bear it, okay?"

"Fine," Harris grumbled. It wasn't really fine, but Troy had a point. He had his wife to think about, and his family. "I'll close my eyes and pretend that they're human if I have to deal with them again."

"Thanks. Now if you'll excuse me, I need to get my own lunch before the mess closes."

The next four weeks passed without incident for him. He did run into several of the lions, or lionesses, actually, a few times, usually in the mess. In each case, they just gave a brief nod, said hello, and avoided him. Troy did tell him later that no one was holding any grudges and that Cassy, the lioness who had precipitated the previous incident, was sorry and sent her apologies.

They'd come out of hyperspace, or whatever it was the scientists called it, two days ago and had another ten days before they'd make it to their destination. He'd noticed everyone was on edge and really had no idea why until the "General Quarters" alarm went off.

"Now hear this! Now hear this! We have a small craft maneuvering to board us! All hands to their security stations! All hands to their security stations! We are about to be boarded!"

There was a loud "clang" then, followed by the sounds of an explosion, and all power briefly went out. Without lights, Harris's office was like a tomb, and he panicked for a moment until the emergency lighting strips came up. They weren't much, but as his eyes adjusted, he could make out enough to see outlines. He heard the tell-tale sounds of the environmental fans start back up, but they sounded a lot more subdued than normal.

He could only assume that they were on emergency power, as well. This was not good! He needed to get back to his berth! He kept his emergency life-support gear there, which he suddenly realized just might be necessary.

Going over to the door, he hit the button to open it, but as expected, with the power out, the door didn't budge. At least he knew how to deal with this. Going to the other side of the door, he opened the "Emergency Release" panel, pulled out the crank for the door, and after disengaging the lock, he quickly cranked it open far enough that he was able to slip out.

Which was when he heard the sounds of gunfire.

They were being attacked.

"Get back into your office!" a husky voice whispered in his ear, and whipping his head around, he saw two of the heavily armed lionesses running down the passageway towards the sounds of the fighting as they quickly disappeared into the darkness.

He shivered for a moment. He hadn't heard them approaching; they'd been that quiet. He thought about returning to his office, but he didn't have his emergency gear there and his berth wasn't really all that far away.

It was also in the direction the two lionesses had come from, not the one where the gunfire was coming from.

The lighting in the passageway was even worse than it had been in his office. He had the distinct impression that someone had removed at least half of what was supposed to be there. Or maybe it was on a different circuit and hadn't come up when the power had gone out?

That made him nervous about just how much damage they may have received when they got boarded. He didn't really know anything about how that worked. He'd heard stories, but surely they didn't just vent the entire hull to vacuum and kill everyone onboard!

He wondered if maybe he should be heading for the life-pods instead of his room, but his emergency life-support gear, which included his pressure suit, was in there, and if they lost atmosphere... Without that, he was dead.

So instead of returning to his office, he hugged the wall, staying out of the center of the hallway to avoid being shot, and slowly made his way to his berth. The gunfire seemed to be moving away, but it was so hard to tell in the metal corridors of the ship as he stopped every few feet to peer into the darkness to try and see what was happening.

He made it past the first intersection without any issues, and then turned left to make his way towards the passage his room was on. It seemed like it'd taken him an eternity to get there, but looking at his tablet, he saw that the ship's power had only gone out a few minutes ago. There were warnings for everyone to shelter in place and stay out of the passageways, but that made no sense to him. What if they lost atmosphere? What if they had to abandon ship?

He was almost to the passageway that his berth was on when the sound of gunfire erupted from it.

He froze. The safety of his berth laid directly ahead, around that corner.

Yet there was fighting going on.

He stood, debating what to do: move forward and peek around the corner, or move back the way he'd come?

What to do?

What to do!

The gunfire increased in volume, and it was moving towards him. Looking around, he tried to figure out what to do, where to run, when a lioness backed around the corner, firing shots back down the passageway.

"I'm slowing them down, there's four of them left in this group. Fighting retreat. Got it. I'll draw them down."

He was surprised he could hear what she was saying, but then again, her rifle wasn't all that loud, compared to the others.

He must have made a noise, because in an instant she was facing him, gun pointed at his head! He gasped and took a step back.

"Shit! I got Harris! He's in the passageway! No, he's not wounded. No, I don't know why he's here!"

"My berth..." he gasped as she turned away from him and fired a few more shots down the passageway she'd just come out of.

"Yeah! Of course we're gonna change plans! I can't leave him here, it's not safe!"

He realized at that moment who it was.

"Cassy?"

"What?" she asked, turning her head to look at him in a flash.

"What's happening?"

"Pirates."

"Pirates! We need to get off the ship!"

"No, I need to get you someplace safe while Sherm and the others close the trap," she said, and turned back towards the hallway. "No, talking to Harris. I can't keep leading them if I gotta evac Harris. What's that? From the port side?"

Harris looked behind him as Cassy looked that way, as well.

"I can't make 'em out yet! Look, I'm gonna have to bug out. I can't risk him getting hurt. What? Yeah, I know it'll hose the plan! If you got any..."

A bullet whizzed by.

"I'm OUT!" Cassy yelled, and he found himself grabbed and yanked off the floor as bullets started coming at him from the hallway behind them. Cassy took off running, a hail of gunfire coming from the other passageway as she crossed in front of him while she pulled him bodily around her left side, then in a bridal carry in front of her as she ran. He didn't miss the grunts as the shots continued, but she was wearing armor, so that'd protect her, he was sure.

"Guess I'm paying for that desert after all!" she grunted as she dashed down the passageway, turning left down the second opening she came to.

"What do you mean they're following me?" he heard her grunt. "Oh," she said, sounding a little dejected.

"What?" he asked.

"They realized I've got a crewmember, and you're obviously important because I've been shielding you with my body," she said, panting.

"I can walk," he blurted out.

"Afraid I'm gonna hurt ya?" she teased, then coughed.

"I'm afraid you're gonna get injured!" he retorted.

"Ya, too late for that," she said, and all but dropped him.

"What do we do?" he asked as she pushed him down the passageway.

"Find a place to wait for help."

"What help?"

"We were moving them to an ambush... But now they're following us...so everyone's gotta move..."

He didn't miss that she was having trouble speaking and was panting heavily. Looking around, he recognized where they were: they were in one of the hallways that led down through the different cargo holds. Stopping, he tried to open one.

"There's no power, we can't get in there," she told him, pushing him away from the hatch.

"There's a manual hatch up ahead on the right," he told her as he remembered the layout.

"It's sealed."

"I have the key."

She stumbled and looked down at him.

"What?"

"I have the key! I'm the purser! It's manual!"

"I'd kiss you, but I'm afraid Sherman would have to kill you," she mumbled.

Harris darted up ahead of her, and pulling the key out of his pocket, he worked the lock and then put his shoulder to the door. A moment after that, Cassy joined him, and the door all but flew open. She fell through the hatch and landed on the floor just as the gunfire started again.

Getting behind it, he slammed into it with all his might. The moment it closed, he spun the locking wheel, engaging it just as someone tried to open it from the other side.

"That was close..." he sighed.

"We're in onna the bays, Harris had a key, I'm gonna take a nap..." he heard Cassy mutter.

Turning to look at her under the muted emergency lighting, he finally noticed that she was covered in blood and there was more of it spreading, slowly, under her.

There was a first-aid kit on the wall, and grabbing it, he dropped to his knees beside her and putting his hands under her, he tried to roll her over unto her stomach.

"I'm not that kinda lioness, Harris," she mumbled, and then giggled.

"Roll over!"

"Sherm'll kill ya, ya know..."

"Roll over, dammit!" He heaved at her body. Who knew lions were so damn heavy?

"Your funeral," she giggled, and heaved herself over as he pushed at her. When she landed on her belly, she went limp, and he worried that she might have died on him. Looking over the back of her armor, it was riddled with holes. She'd been shot protecting him.

"Dammit," he swore, and opening the first-aid kit, he started using the bandages inside to plug the holes. He needed to get her out of her armor and wasn't sure how to do it. It was strapped on. He could see that because the piece on her right side had shattered from a couple of hits she'd taken there. Looking her over, he saw she had a knife on her hip, and drawing it, he started cutting through the straps.

As he got through each one, he found a few more he had to cut as well. Thankfully, the blade was sharp; it helped him to make quick work of the fabric holding the plates.

Flipping the back plate off, he paled at the mass of wounds on her back. Grabbing the first-aid kit, he went to work, trying to remember everything he'd ever been taught about treating wounds. No one had taught him what to do for people who'd been shot, but hopefully, if he could stop the bleeding, she'd live long enough for help to get there.

He had no idea how long he'd been working on her back when the lights all came back on. A moment after that, someone was pounding on the door.

"Harris! Open up!" he could hear a very deep voice yelling from the other side.

Jumping to his feet, he disengaged the lock, then got knocked to the side as the door flew open and Sherman jumped into the room. If at all possible, he looked even bigger than before. He took one look at Cassy lying on the floor and all of the bandages on her, swore loudly, then picking her up like she didn't weigh a thing, he bolted out the door and was gone.

Sighing, Harris leaned back against the wall and slowly slid down until he was sitting on his ass.

"Are you okay over there?" another lioness that he recognized as Anna said, stepping inside.

"I'm fine," Harris sighed. "I really messed things up, didn't I?" He shook his head.

"Sure looks like you were doing okay from all those bandages you used."

"I meant, if I had stayed put like I was told by those two who saw me in the hallway, she wouldn't have gotten shot trying to save my dumb ass."

Anna shrugged. "Why didn't you stay put?"

"My emergency gear is all in my berth. When they took out the power, I was worried about ending up in a vacuum."

"Oh! Sorry!" Anna said, looking embarrassed.

"What do you have to be sorry about?"

"We had engineering pull all of the power when they breached us and came aboard. It's easier for us if they can't see so well. We're cats. Seeing in the dark is no biggie."

"Don't they have night vision?"

"Most pirates can't afford it, but even if they do, it makes a high-pitched whine that we can all hear, so it still helps us find 'em."

Harris shook his head again. "You got the pirates?"

"Oh, we got 'em, all right," Anna said, a predatory look on her face. "We got 'em good."

Harris was sure he didn't want to know. Looking over at where Cassy had been laying, there was a mess of blood, bandage wrappers and other things.

"I guess I should clean up that mess," he said, motioning to the spot. "Please let me know how Cassy is doing."

"You sure?"

"Yeah," he nodded, "I'm sure. I'm sorry I got her shot."

"Okay." With that, she was gone.

⁂

"Sherman's been looking for you," Troy said, coming into Harris's office as he went over the list of repairs the ship would need and trying to itemize the list of parts and items they'd need so he could forward it all to the company offices before they docked.

"I know, I've been hiding from him," Harris said with a slight shiver.

"Still don't like the animals?" Troy said, giving him a sour look.

"I got his wife shot! More like I'm afraid of what he's going to do to me!" Troy replied harshly.

"Why would he do anything to you?"

"Why wouldn't he? I shouldn't have been out there! If I hadn't, she wouldn't have had to risk her life to save me! My fears and my own stupidity is to blame, not those damn pirates. I'm just glad she survived, or I'd be a dead man for sure."

Troy blinked. "Wait, you think he's after you because you got her wounded?"

"Wouldn't you be if it was your wife?" Harris shot back.

"Hmm. That's a good question. Anna told us you thought the pirates had blown the power out and we were going to lose atmosphere."

"So?"

"So no one thought to tell you that's what we do when we get hit by pirates. Then again, no one thought we'd get hit again so soon."

"What's that supposed to mean?"

"Your predecessor quit because we got hit on the edge of your system, on the way in. Was too much for her, so she quit the moment we docked."

Harris sighed and shook his head. "Then thank goodness for the lions, because they've saved everyone twice now." Harris looked away for a moment, then making up his mind, he looked back at Troy. "Look, I fucked up. I realize that now. I made a big mistake, and I insulted the very people whom we rely on to keep us all safe. If the captain wants me off the ship, I won't protest it."

"The captain doesn't want you off the ship, and I'm not looking to hurt you," came a deep voice from the open hatch behind Troy.

Harris could see Sherman standing there. Anna and one of his other wives were with him. They weren't geared up and were wearing just their shipsuits, but they were still big, and Sherman was still huge. The suit wasn't hiding the size of his biceps, which were probably larger than Harris's thighs.

"I'm sorry, Sherman," Harris said. "I'm really truly sorry."

"You didn't know," Sherman said with a shrug. "And protecting you is why we're here. Besides, *you're* not the one who shot her. She also wasn't the only one who got wounded. But that's not why I'm here."

"Oh?"

"You saved her life. If you hadn't gotten her armor off and stopped the bleeding, she would have died. That's why I'm here. I want to thank you for saving her life, even though you don't like us."

"It's not that I don't like you," Harris said, looking embarrassed.

"It's not?"

"It's that you scare the hell out of me! I don't claim to be a brave man, Sherman, and Cassy could easily break me in two! Like a lot of folks, I don't like things that scare me. I don't like being afraid."

"Then why did you bandage Cassy?" one of the other lionesses asked.

"Because she saved my life, and I didn't want anyone to think I was a coward."

"Fair enough."

Sherman nodded. "Just understand that as far as my pride and the other two are concerned, you're our friend now. I don't know if that means much to you, but if you ever need one of us to help you with anything, don't hesitate to ask—we'll be there."

Harris smiled and nodded. "Thank you."

"And you're gonna get hugged by each of us the next time we see you in the lunchroom," Anna said and grinned. "Fair warning!"

Harris just nodded and watched as they all turned and left.

"So," Troy said after a minute, "change your mind, have you?"

"They still scare me," Harris admitted. "But not so much that I'm going to avoid them anymore, or reject their friendship."

"You know what they say about a man with a bunch of lions for friends, don't you?"

Harris shook his head no.

Troy grinned. "A man like that...well, he's not afraid of anything."

END

From Raconteur Press

Ghosts of Malta

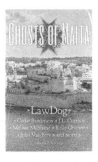

Knights of Malta

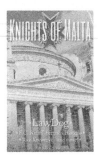

Saints of Malta

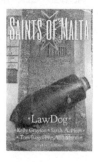

Falcons of Malta

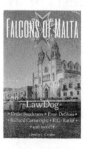

Space Cowboys

Space Cowboys 2: Electric Rodeo

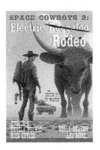

Space Marines

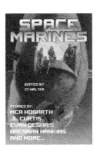

Space Marines 2

Postcards From Mars

Steam-Powered Postcards

Fanta-Fly Postcards

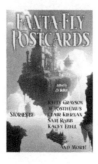

Postcards From Foolz

Single Servings of Liberty

Made in the USA
Monee, IL
16 August 2023

41132757R00125